Man of the Fields

Fields

The Next Crusade for Salem

Henry F. Wilde

Preface

Dear Reader,

This book is not meant to harm or denounce any
particular faiths, groups of people, or specific individuals. It is
not meant to shame Catholics, modern-day pagans, or any
religious groups. This book is an allegory. It is a mirror. It is
meant to be a reflection of our world and its history through
symbolism, storytelling, and art. It reflects our world's past,
present, and possible future. This book features religious and
political themes that may be sensitive to some readers. This book
is a passion project that is meant to represent my distaste for the
relationship between religion and politics within our society. I
ask you to please read this book with an open mind and heart.

Sincerely,

Henry F. Wilde

1

Dark the night was. Cold and damp. 1917, the year of our Lord. Lightning flashed, illuminating the dark, gloomy halls of the Vatican. The carpets were blood red and gnashed in anger as a holy father scurried to the bed chambers of the Holy Prince. The priest tripped on his long, gray robes and fell to the cold ground. Lightning flashed again, and the light slightly distorted his vision for a few moments. He swore at himself for his clumsiness. He clutched his crucifix, which hung around his neck tightly in his big, sweaty hands. Praying for strength and swiftness, he resumed his urgent scurry. News had to be delivered this dark evening. Terrible news.

The holy father made it towards the entrance of the sacred bed chambers of the prince. Two tall, brutish, masked men dressed in red armored uniforms guarded the large iron doors. They were armed with swords. They positioned themselves ready and armed as the priest approached them.

"What business do you bring, Father?" gruffly asked one of the guards. He clutched the hilt of his sword, preparing to draw it from its sheath. The priest brought up his hands in fear.

"I have brought fateful news for the Holy Prince tonight," the priest said, holding a red letter sealed in gold wax. The guard took the envelope, opened it, and read its contents. His eyes widened. The guards stood back and opened the heavy, ironed doors. The gentlemen heaved as they opened the doors, slightly grunting despite possessing their brutish muscular stature. The father scurried into the room.

The room was white, elegant, and regal. Marble possessed every corner of the room and essential and priceless works of art. Greek nudes stood unmoving in their portraits and busts. Their gentle curvatures enticed the human eye into desire and awe for such perfect detail of the female or male form. The bed itself was a masterpiece with regal, expensive silk sheets. The extended canopy was strung with lush, soft greens as vibrant as the Amazons. In bed, sleeping peacefully, was the Holy Prince himself, Lorenzo Bartolomeo.

The father stood awkwardly at the foot of the prince's bed as the holy man snored in his pillow. He feared the prince's anger for disturbing his slumber, but the priest's news was far more critical. He thought of tapping the prince's shoulder or slightly shaking him, but he feared that the prince was to assume the priest was attacking him. He cleared his throat and said in a somewhat loud voice,

"Excuse me, my holy liege...."

Immediately, the prince awoke. Lorenzo rubbed his crusty eyes. Lorenzo Bartolomeo was the Holy Imperial Prince of the Holy Inquisitional Nations under the name of the holy Catholic Church. In his early 60s, he had a wrinkled, frowned face and short white hair. The prince was the son of the Holy Imperial Emperor, Francesco Bartolomeo. As a prince, he patiently waits for the day his father passes and attains the ruler of the nations throughout Europe. He is stern and harsh towards his citizens, just as his father had taught him and his father before him. He maintains the correct traditions Christ had taught His disciples. The proper ways of the Catholic nations. He is responsible for keeping the foreign, unholy defilement away from his people. He

3

sat up and peered at the foot of his bed. He turned on a nearby lamp and saw the worried priest.

"What is it, Father? Why have you awakened me at such a ridiculous hour? So ridiculous that it cannot wait until the morning," he grunted as he sat upon his feathered pillows. The priest heard a ruffling underneath the prince's bed sheets. The prince growled in annoyance. He quickly opened his blankets as if unwrapping a Christmas present. Instead of toys, two young naked women slept under the satin sheets. He violently slapped them both.

"GET OUT, YOU FILTHY HARLOTS," he roared as they clutched their bare breasts and naked buttocks and ran out the bedroom door. The prince's courtesans had spent the evening with him. The priest stood embarrassed for a moment but continued.

"My Holy Prince, I am displeased to inform you that the Holy Imperial Emperor has been murdered this evening."

Lorenzo's eyes widened in disbelief. He then sat at the edge of his bed, looking towards the white marble floor. A single tear shed, and the prince immediately wiped it. He slowly turned to his messenger.

"How could this happen? What in the blazes happened?" Lorenzo asked sourly.

"My lord…your father has been found dead in one of the most…displeasing ways," shuttered the small priest. "One of his caretakers entered his room to give him his nightly medication. She saw that he was not in bed. She then looked up and saw him in one of the most appalling conditions…."

"Enough of this soft language! I demand to see my father! Bring me to him!"

"But my lord, you will be most uncomfortable…."

"Do not tell me what I can or cannot handle, priest. I am your emperor now, and I demand you to show me to my father's chambers."

"As you wish, my…emperor."

Lorenzo was then dressed by his caretakers. His caretakers were all young and beautiful, but their faces were covered as a sign of modesty. Caretakers were used for other purposes considered taboo to mention in the eyes of the Holy

Vatican. The beautiful women carefully and delicately dressed Lorenzo in his expensive exotic robes. He grew annoyed by their slow dressing, violently pushed one who was presenting his right sleeve, and put his arm through the socket himself. He shook his hand away irritably to dismiss them. His caretakers bowed respectfully and left the chamber. Lorenzo exited his chamber and was led by eight guards that circled around him as he paced towards his father's chambers across the other side of the Vatican Palace. When he finally reached the bed chambers, he pushed away his guards and opened the door.

Briskly, agents surrounding the room turned their heads and bowed in reverence. There were approximately twenty agents in the room. They all wore armored black uniforms and brandished the cross symbol of their order. Their faces were covered by a mask that would terrify the bravest soul. Only their eyes showed through a tiny horizontal slit. Since birth, they had been training to fight for the glory of God and protect the Holy Catholic Inquisitional Nations. The agents were trained in advanced hand-to-hand combat, knew the Holy Word backward and forwards, and possessed extensive knowledge of medieval

6

torture to achieve information. They were trained to give their lives for the citizens of the Nations. If they died, they would be venerated as martyrs. They were the Hammer of Witches or known by ordinary folk as HOWs.

The agents were sprawled around the room, taking photographs of the scene. The prince pushed past various agents that saluted for their royal leader. Lorenzo looked at the emperor's bed and covered his mouth in shock.

Lorenzo fell to his knees. He folded his hands and prayed, weeping softly.

One of the lead agents approached Lorenzo and brought him to his feet. "My lord, based on the evidence of our emperor's murder, it is a clear and sly strike from the enemy," the agent stated. "My fellow agents suspect the assassin to have disguised herself as a caretaker and murdered the emperor when they were alone. My liege, these strange markings on his flesh are ancient runes of the devil. I am afraid that they have infiltrated the Vatican and murdered our most holy emperor. The witches have killed the emperor."

Lorenzo's face reddened in a fury. His eyes bulged, and he ground his teeth with all his might. He bit the side of his cheek until it bled viciously, and he could taste it. He spat on the floor. He turned away from the corpse and the surrounding agents. He slammed his fist on a nearby table. A decorative vase clattered in place, causing the small priest to jump in fright.

"This ends tonight," he growled. "We, the holy Catholic Church, have done nothing to exterminate the hags of the American continent. We have done nothing to avenge the firstborns of our people, the children murdered in the name of Satan. I will not allow this anymore! Tomorrow, I will be crowned Holy Imperial Emperor of the Holy Catholic Inquisitional Nations! My forefathers were too weak to strike a blow against them! My own father was too weak and was killed as a result! This is a sign from God that he has bestowed onto me the flaming sword to strike upon and slay the Devil and his wicked followers! He has given me the mighty power to annihilate them! We now have the technology and power to obliterate those hags. We now can put our army to good use! We shall destroy the American witch-breed and burn them all to hell!"

"But, sire," nervously mumbled the priest. "How will we destroy the American witches?"

"We have a war to win. We will be in dire need of a professional in the circumstances such as these. Commander Octavian," said Lorenzo. The agent saluted his emperor. "You will be heading to South Africa tonight. I have someone you need to find."

2

The sun smiled upon the South African lands, dry and barren. Heat radiated from the dried savannah. Few antelope play and dance nowadays. The dusty, heated wind blew at the faces of Johannesburg. Johannesburg greeted the sun with an unwelcome bitterness. Water has been scarce for the past two hundred years, ever since the war began. The people of Johannesburg stood outside of their huts. Once a capital place of enslavement, it was now an abandoned, unloved wasteland. Water was rare and the land was fruitless. African children played games in the dusty, barren fields as a strapping young Italian man tinkered with his metal contraption.

Sweat dripped down Arturo's brow as he fastened a bolt. He wiped it with his colorful handkerchief, which was given to him as a gift from the village women. Sweat soaked his dress shirt and dust-caked his best dress pants and overalls. The heat was unbearable, but he continued working. His mustache quivered in excitement. He was almost finished with the contraption he had been working on for the past three weeks. Today, he would bring water to the humble people of Johannesburg.

"Doc! Doc! Doc!" shouted the young African children. They all ran towards Arturo, distinguishing curiosity, and awe in their little eyes. They were curious about his progress with the contraption. The machine puffed and smoked. Innocence illuminated within their little hearts. Arturo smiled to himself as the children approached and watched him work.

"Doc, are you still building our machine?" asked a young boy.

"Yes, Brave. It is almost done soon! I think I will be finishing it today," smiled Arturo, as he sat up to chat with the children.

"What are you using the machine for, Doc?" inquisitively asked a little girl.

"It is to bring you water, Imka," cooed Arturo. "That way, your mamma and baba can make food for your grandmother, grandfather, brothers, and sisters. And your bellies can become

11

nice and full!" He smiled and playfully poked at her belly. Imka then giggled at Arturo's silliness. Laughter was rare in Johannesburg. He marveled and felt complete to hear such joy. It had been months since he has heard anyone laugh in barren South Africa.

Arturo tinkered his shining contraption. The machine was gargantuan. It shined a silver shine in the afternoon sunlight. He grew excited as the children watched from a distance. He whispered a quick and silent prayer and pulled the switch. The machine began to vibrate and hum with life. The engine groaned loudly. Steam spewed from the machine's sides, whistling to the children. The children covered their ears and giggled. Arturo laughed in excitement and ran towards the back of the great gizmo. Soon, all the villagers came to witness Arturo's latest work. The village women, who held their babies, watched closely and carefully. The village men watched defensively from the back of the crowd. At the same time, the elders glared in judgment and fascination with Arturo. Arturo brought a tin bucket and held it underneath a faucet. He twisted the faucet open. Fresh, cool water gushed out in no time as it filled the pail to the very brim. The village people clapped and praised. Arturo has given Johannesburg the first working water system in decades.

As a Traveler, Arturo's mission was to bring prosperity and hospitable livelihood to the village of Johannesburg. Travelers had served Johannesburg for centuries. He and a few other Travelers had built homes, vehicles, and irrigation systems to the very fringes of South Africa. Arturo saw goodness and hope within the dying city while the Church was policing the rest of the world. He saw joy, love, and peace. He saw true potential from the two of three years he had served his mission here. Under his wishes and prayers, Arturo desired to bring hope to the hearts of South Africa.

Arturo smiled as the people of Johannesburg celebrated. His mustache tickled his lips as he smiled. The children sang and danced with joy. Quickly, all the women of the tribe brought their clay jars and filled them with water, bringing them to their homes and families. Satisfaction and joy swelled within Arturo.

"Arturo, you surprise me every single day!" laughed a voice from behind. "First the new buses, now running water. All I can do is build a nice house for them."

"Oh hush now, Pino! I would never have completed it if you didn't help me get the parts I needed," Arturo candidly stated.

Pino was Arturo's closest friend and a long time Traveler. He was tall, young, but quiet. He had long, wavy, blonde hair. Pino was well-built and had a heart of gold. Pino never told anyone where he came from. He brandished a thin scar across his right eyebrow despite his good looks, although he wore round specs to cover it.

"You're a funny chump, my old boy. How did you do it?"

"The machine extracts the dry air, turns it into moisture, and converts it to fresh, clean water. This was possibly my hardest project yet. I'm ready to build cars again, my dear boy. Like God, I shall rest until Sunday."

"As will I, Arturo! I was starting to get worried that the communion wine would be the only thing the people of

Johannesburg were going to drink! We best try to avoid that problem."

"That reminds me! We must find a better hiding spot for the communion wine because some boys have been stealing it and been mixing it to make hooch. Pray for strength for me, please."

"*Benedictus pacis*, my brother," Arturo laughed. "Any word from the Church? It's been months since they've sent equipment and supplies to us."

"I've written to them constantly, Arturo. I haven't received a response."

"If we don't get supplies soon, the village will tear us to pieces. We might need to contact the Namibian black market dealers again for more supplies."

"Good plan because the chief is growing more and more impatient. I'll be sure to have the other brothers hide the women and children if they ask for any trades or services. Any word from Antonietta or the kids?"

Arturo's heart skipped a beat. The sun burned the top of his neatly combed dark hair as he nervously continued pacing back to his hut. Pino followed him. Sadness and homesickness overcame him. He inhaled deeply and sighed.

"I haven't heard from them either," Arturo stated somberly, as he grabbed a bucket for himself, filling it with water. "It's been weeks since I've received a letter. I sent the kids little wind-ups and a letter for Antonietta. I hope they are doing alright, brother. *Benedictus pacis*."

Pino and Arturo entered the hut. The temperature instantly dropped from the blazing heat to a relaxed and comfortable temperature. Goosebumps rose on their skin in response, allowing the hairs on their neck and arms to elevate. Makeshift fans were hung from each room corner, just as they were for every other hut. A small wooden desk stood on one side, a small coffee table and two chairs in the east, and a small, unkempt cot on the far right.

"Please make yourself at home, Pino," Arturo said, motioning for Pino to sit in a chair. "Coffee?"

"No, please, Arturo. Let me take care of it. Sit down and relax," said Pino, calmly sitting his friend down.

"Thank you, old boy."

Pino got out the crushed coffee beans and poured them into the filter. He ran the fresh water from his bucket and pressed the button. The machine purred and steamed slightly. Pino poured a cup for Arturo and himself. Pino handed the small clay cup to Arturo. The very smell of his drink entered his nostrils and brought Arturo energy. He took a small sip and savored its bittersweet flavor. It had been days since he slept. Coffee was much needed.

"Arturo, can I ask you something?"

"Of course, my dear boy," Arturo said as he fought to keep his heavy eyes open. Now that his project has been completed, exhaustion overcame him like a wave in the ocean.

"You have been a Traveler for two years now. And you have helped the people of Johannesburg tremendously. You've brought cars, air conditioning, houses and now water. You've brought nothing but goodness and prosperity to these people. You truly belong here. But I must ask you: do you miss your family?"

Arturo looked at the ground and sat silently for a moment. The two could only hear the fans whirring in motion. Arturo sighed again.

"Every day, Pino. Every day. Every day I miss Antonietta and the kids. I'd do anything to see them again. I'd do anything to kiss my wife and children again, but I was sent here to help these good people. I feel accomplished by doing something. I am giving back to a group of people that have been taken away from a decent livelihood. The priests of Europe sit comfortably in their castles. The village has been enslaved for centuries by our ancestors, old boy. God sent me here to create, not destroy. Today, I made one of the children laugh! I haven't heard a burst of single laughter or seen a smile in ages! I want to continue bringing joy and happiness to these people. I want to save lives, not destroy them as our Church does. It is our mission, brother. But to see my family, I would give my own life to see them again."

"And our mission will be complete soon, my dear boy," said Pino, patting Arturo's shoulder. "You will hear from

Antonietta soon, brother. Have no fear. With your help, we will save the people of South Africa in no time! *Benedictus pacis.*"

Arturo smiled at Pino and took another sip of his coffee. A loud commotion came from the outside. The sounds of engines bellowed in the far distance. Arturo's smile disappeared. Pino and Arturo rushed outside of the hut. Mothers and fathers stood outside their huts, embracing their children in fear. In the distance, three ominous black trucks rolled, leaving a trail of dust behind them in the wind. Their engines roared, instilling terror within the South African people. Arturo fixed his hair and curled his mustache. The trucks all stopped at once in a single file line. They were the Hammers of Witches.

A tall individual stepped out of the tall, ominous vehicle. He wore an all-black armored uniform, only brandishing his eyes and buzzed salt-pepper hair. The man had hawk-like silver eyes that could slice the gazer's throat in a single glance. He was muscular and stood approximately six feet and several inches tall. On his belt held a pistol and a spiked truncheon. His heavy boots crunched the ground as he marched viciously towards Arturo and Pino.

"Are you Dr. Arturo Mattei?" gruffly asked the armored man in all black.

Arturo was struck with bewilderment by the militant individual who stood before him. He swallowed his fear. "Indeed I am. And whom am I speaking with, sir? And what brings you here?"

"I am Commander James Octavian. We will answer your questions soon. We have much to discuss. Please take us to your place of residence immediately," aggressively ordered the commander.

Arturo, followed by Pino, Commander Octavian, and two other soldiers armed with assault weapons, marched to the hut. The two soldiers stood guard outside the hut's entrance. The commander cleared the table, pushing off a bowl of fruit and coffee mugs to the ground. Arturo and Pino stood awkwardly as the dangerous commando viciously rearranged the kitchen and propped up a device.

"Dr. Mattei, just last night, the Holy Imperial Emperor, Francesco Bartolomeo, was murdered under the hands of the fiendish hag breed," stated Octavian. "We have gathered evidence from our superiors, and are most definitely certain that witches from America have successfully assassinated our emperor."

An image of the deceased emperor flashed before their eyes from the device. Arturo's eyes widened in shock, and a pit formed below his stomach. Pino nervously began shaking, clenching his fists in anxious anger. The horrific image burned into their very soul. Octavian continued.

"The emperor was found in his sacred dormitory hung upside down on a cross, above his headboard." Soon he revealed a graphic close-up of the emperor's face. Reddish greenish puss dripped from his mouth and ears in a horrific stance. "One can see the multiple wounds and brands given by the witch assassin." His body hung loosely open as if it were a marionette, waiting for its master to bring it back to life. Blood and mucus were seen to exude from the victim's mouth. His teeth and lips were a dark red, and his tongue fell lifelessly. His body was shriveled like ancient papyrus and was branded by runes and symbols of unknown origin. Arturo knew that they were the marks of something sinister.

"Commander, why have you come here to reveal this classified information? This is way beyond my expertise...." asked Arturo.

"Dr. Mattei, because we have been at war for hundreds of years with the witch enemy. We must take matters into our own hands and assert our dominance over the devilish country for assassinating our holy commander. With God's mighty fist, we must bring you to the fight. To bring you to our holy war."

"But why me, Commander? I am nothing but a simple Traveler. I have been serving on my mission here in Johannesburg for two years, and it is my mission to bring peace to the good people of Johannesburg. After all, I will be reunited with my family once again. Why do I have to be a part of all this?"

"Dr. Mattei, you have come from a long line of inventors. Your family has helped the holy Catholic Church for centuries. Your family has enhanced our civilization with your advanced technology. You have brought us tanks, aeroplanes, automobiles. And Dr. Mattei...we know you possess something that you have been keeping from the Holy See for some time now."

Arturo nervously turned around and looked outside of the hut window. He anxiously fidgeted with his wedding band. It was gold, scratched, but still shined like the day he forged it. It had an eloquent design with foliage and a simple finishing Tau τ. A wave of regret swelled his heart and fell to his stomach. He couldn't breathe. He had feared this day would come.

"With the device, Dr. Mattei, we can solidify the power of Christ and expel the devilish continent once and for all. Your device is the only power we possess to end this war. Think of the millions of lives you will save! Avenge your emperor! Think of Christ! Christ must prevail. You are the warrior, and we are the hammer. We must strike now before they strike again."

"Can I be frank with you, Commander? It was purely out of drunken genius when I made that unholy trinket. I wanted to selfishly end everything–all my pain and suffering, but I found hope and goodness. I came here to Johannesburg to give life, not take it away. That is why I joined my brotherhood, Commander.

We must pray for peace, and fight with peace. I refuse to come with you, good sir. And with that, I apologize."

There was an ominous silence that entered the room. One could only hear the hum of the fans as they provided fresh cool air throughout the quaint hut. Octavian sighed through his mask, and his silver eyes reflected a piercing fury of impatience and anger.

"I think you forgot your place, Doctor," gritted the commander. "As a loyal citizen of the Church, you must follow your commands given not only by myself but by the new Holy Emperor himself. Not to mention we have your wife and children in custody, Doctor. It would be a shame to allow the Vatican authorities to…handle your family in our care. You are aware of how the Church handles those who do not obey the authority of Our Holy Father. Aren't you, Dr. Mattei?"

A lump formed in Arturo's throat. He looked at a picture frame that hung by the hut window. His family smiled at him, encouraging him. Thoughts of his family swindled in his imagination. Thoughts of his beautiful wife and children, playing with them in the countryside of Cassino. He pictured playing

24

catch with his two boys and smiling at his darling Antonietta, who picked flowers with their young daughters. The girls picked flowers and made a crown for their mother. Antonietta radiated with beauty and happiness. Her smile sang Arturo a song of passion and content. How he missed his sweet family. He looked at Pino, who had turned pale from fright. He swallowed his pride. Arturo knew what the Church was capable of. He had heard stories of capital punishment. Hangings, gas chambers, and drownings were only a few of thousands of the methods the Church had performed and perfected throughout the centuries. Losing his family would mean losing everything. He would do anything for his family.

"What is it that I have to do, Commander?" quietly asked Arturo. The painful pit in Arturo's stomach worsened. The commander clicked on the device, and a map appeared. It was a hologram featuring a detailed map of North America.

"We will send our ships to the east coast of the continent," stated the Commander. "You will be escorted by my men and will be sent to the nation's capital, Salem. There you and my men will infiltrate the capital building..."

An image of a glorious yet crumbling castle appeared. The court had few windows but was dimly lit by candlelight. The castle was massive, gloomy, and entwined with deep woodlands. The trees were dark, twisted, and violent by nature. They grew huge, strong branches that no ax or machinery could possibly cut or scrape. The trunks stood against any element that came to challenge them. Although the ancient castle appeared weak, it was supported by the enchanted forest. Arturo studied the castle, silently scaling and rebuilding the structure. A prick of interest and curiosity slightly consumed him. He felt a sort of calling to learn more about this place and those who inhabited it.

"...and there you will detonate the device. The main objective of this mission, Doctor, is to conquer, detonate and evacuate. We will then send in our troops after the bomb is detonated, attack the entire east coast, and move westward. With your help, Doctor, we will solidify our position in this holy war, avenge the emperor and bring justice to the Church."

The hologram's image shifted. The device displayed an animated image of the castle and the surrounding forest. There, little huts and houses surrounded the castle. A red dot blinked seven times in the middle of the castle. In seconds, the red dot expanded, devouring all of the castle's surroundings. A lifeless, green title saying "Mission Complete" blinked dully on the screen.

Arturo shuttered and felt a dark presence up his spine. Despite the cold air blowing at his face, he felt warm and anxious. He felt the pit in his stomach grow and quiver in his body. It convulsed and came alive. It consumed his intestines and grabbed hold of his heart, ready to make it its next meal. He felt his breath grow shallow. The creature clawed its way up Arturo's throat and held his tongue. He was unable to speak. Shame and fear were the only possessions that stood at his side. He swallowed the best he could and slowly muttered to the Commander, "I accept your mission, Commander. With your permission, may you please leave my brother and me alone in my hut? I have to pack my things for my journey."

"Very well, Dr. Mattei. You have twenty minutes to pack all of your belongings," stated the Commander. The Commander then clicked his heavy black boots, marched out, and roughly slammed the hut door.

3

Arturo looked out the window and waited for the Commander to leave at a respectable distance. He then covered his face with his hands and sighed. Arturo reached for his breast pocket and brought out a small smoking pipe. He opened a small container and filled the pipe's chamber with tobacco. He then took a match and lit the tobacco pieces. The chamber gave a light poof, and the blaze ignited brightly. Arturo took a few puffs at the side of his lips and blew a cloud of smoke lightly. A few wisps of smoke escaped his nose as if he were a medieval dragon snoozing and guarding his gold. He savored the flavor of his pipe. His eyes were red and tired from lack of sleep. Exhausted and lost, he smoked his pipe as he sat in his chair. He looked out the window and saw the children of Johannesburg chasing each other in fun. They laughed. He smiled. Joy was flourishing, as did their new water. A wave of sadness continuously lingered as he saw the African children play. Happiness was nowhere to be found in the hut.

Pino took a chair and sat at the table with Arturo. He took a cigarette from his pocket and lit it with Arturo's match. He smoked a few puffs. The cigarette was bitter yet relaxed him. The smoke fogged his glasses slightly. He then took a handkerchief from his breast pocket and polished the frames. He then took the remaining bud and pressed it on the ashtray. Ashes danced and crawled in the tray. One spark bit Pino on his finger. He quickly moved his finger away and sucked on it to cool it off. It left no mark but still felt painful. He sighed.

"It's going to be alright, old boy. I promise," attempted Pino in an optimistic and peaceful tone. "You will for sure be safe under the authority of the commander. He and his men are strong. You'll complete this mission in no time and come home to your family! It's going to be quite alright, brother. But please tell me, Doc, what is this device?"

Arturo continued puffing his pipe. He nervously tapped his foot, staring at the empty table. A simple, sturdy table made from the dead acacia trees grew near the village. It was plain, beautiful, yet empty. Only two chairs sat on opposite sides. The two men of God sat. Arturo looked up at his good friend with wild eyes.

"Pino, I must tell you that, at the time, I had no comprehension of the catastrophic danger this device would possess. I am a Mattei. I have come from a long line of inventors and soldiers of the Church. My family is responsible for the modern technologies and successes of the Church. My father and his father before him changed the modern world forever and became supporters of the campaign against all heretics and traitors of the Church. We were warriors. Men of metal. We were holy knights.

My brother, Roberto, was a knight. Under the emperor, he was asked to secretly command an attack in Northern America—a desolate, unforgiving land of ice and snow. I, worried about my brother's safety, volunteered to join my brother in his conquest of America. I was young, only seventeen years old. I was scared. My brother smiled and shed not one drop of fear. He was fearless, my brother. Roberto was determined to bring victory to the Church. Despite his heroic behavior, he was patient and encouraging with me. Shaking in my boots, I shivered as I sat in the submarine, waiting for my death. He pulled me by the arm and held me. He assured me, 'Everything will be OK, old sport. We'll be home in no time at all.'

He then pulled from under his black armored uniform a golden device. It was circular, light, yet simple. He handed it to me. There was a small, ridged button on the very top of it. I clicked it. It was a pocket watch. There were beautiful arabesque designs of vines that spiraled on the face of the eye. The watch's ornate bronze remained motionless. He then said to me, 'I got this on my tour in Israel. I bought it in the marketplace. I loved it so much. Little did I realize, the clock never worked! I could've given the simp who sold me the damn watch a piece of my mind, but I loved the watch so damn much. But I want you to have it, old boy. You deserve it.'

At the dead of night, our sub surfaced near the shores of what was once known as the Chesapeake Bay. My brother commanded his platoon to immediately exit the submarine. The windy sea froze us to the very core. Despite our thick armor, we shivered like leaves. The cold wind bit our faces. The icy sand froze my boots. I shivered in anxious fear and bitter coldness. The elements were already against us. However, I held my gun and moved on. Roberto gave us the signal to continue. Our platoon, tightly positioned in a guerilla fashion, stepped into the winded deep forest at the end of the beach. The forest was dark and dense. Even in the moonlight, we could barely see past our hands, yet we journeyed on. We silently mushed on, trying our best to avoid making loud crunching footsteps in the snow. We continued heading west until my brother motioned us to stop.

In the distance, he saw a faint golden light from a firelight. It was a village. Children and women were dancing around the tall, gigantic fire. You could hear the roaring as the flames danced with the nude women and children. Drums rhythmically hummed, and string instruments loomed in the distance. The people all wore masks and animal skins, yet they were all naked. Despite the bitter dead of winter, they pranced around the fire as if it were the hottest day of summer. They all laughed and cackled and sang strange hymns on the top of their lungs. It was the night of the Devil. They were all his children. They were witches.

A loud snap suddenly came from behind us. We all turned at once to investigate. We couldn't see what was behind us. We then turned back, and the music had stopped. I looked into my telescope. The villagers had vanished. We then heard the caw of a raven. We turned and pointed our weapons in its direction. We heard a distant snap of a twig. Silence hung in the air like an icicle. Serene but potentially dangerous.

Suddenly, three soldiers levitated and were thrown across the rugged, snowy brush like rag dolls. Blood splattered upon impact. The men's flesh began to melt. They screamed bloody murder, begging for their lives. They clawed their faces as their flesh oozed and hissed. We then looked up at naked men and women waving their hands, whispering chants in unison, clinging to the trees like a flock of birds. Quietly they sang their ungodly hymns. Their eyes glowed green in the night. Our men then opened fire in the trees. Nimbly and savagely, they dodged our bullets, yet we fought with all our might. By the will of God, we would end this witch breed and seize the day. Roberto fought valiantly beside me. He and I shot our weapons at the enemy to the best of our capability. One by one, the witches were shot down from their perches. We were seemingly victorious. Like King David against Goliath, we were small yet mighty. Blood smeared our faces as the casualties increased. Nude, bloodied corpses lay in the snow.

A witch levitated from her perch. Her feet gently touched the blood-stained snow. She was young, had blonde hair, and was beautiful. Her hair was so blonde that it merely matched the snow. She had a small nose and had the bluest eyes. She was short in stature. Her beauty was mesmerizing as she stood naked in the gentle snow. I stared into her eyes and pointed my weapon toward her. All the gunfire seemed to have stopped. Time slowed as she moved closer to me. She walked closer and closer. Her feet delicately made an imprint on the snow. She elegantly motioned towards me like a gentle doe, looking at me with her innocent gaze. She touched the barrel of my machine gun and lowered it to the ground. I felt safe and secure. I felt at peace. Peace at last.

'Arturo, no!' my brother shouted. Time seemed to have caught up to me because everything moved so quickly. I looked up at the witch, who smiled, and with incredible agility, she

34

grabbed me by the neck and threw me against a nearby tree. I hit my head and immediately tasted blood. My vision blurred as I lay on the ground. My ears rang, and I felt incredibly dizzy. I slowly moved toward cover and crawled behind a tree trunk. I saw Roberto sparring with my assailant. However, she was far too quick for him. She snatched his machine gun and threw it to the ground. He pulled out his knife and swung it quickly, but she was far too fast. She levitated once again. She then kicked him in the square of his back, and he fell with a big "oof." Roberto pulled out a grenade from his front pouch. He looked at me, terrified. His eyes were filled with love and regret. He then closed his eyes and pulled the pin.

BOOOOOOOOOOOOM!!!

My ears rang, and my vision was blurred once again. Debris, blood, and fire flew all around the perimeter where my brother stood. Nothing but a giant crater surrounded by fire and blood. My eyes adjusted. My mouth felt dry, and I felt nothing. I continued to stare where my brother once stood. I felt empty and numb. I looked around and saw nothing but fallen soldiers and witches. I was the only survivor. I went to the small crater, and I cried. I cried harder than I had ever cried before. I lost my brother. He was gone–never to be seen again.

I then carried myself and trudged back to the icy shores of the Chesapeake, returning to my vessel. Only the captain and sailors of the sub remained on the ship. I quickly waved to the boat as I ran. The medic thankfully tended my wounds, but I was speechless. My eyes were wide, and I felt numb. The only thing I heard, or saw was the explosion. Over and over...."

As Arturo finished his story, the hut door then burst open. Both men turned while smoking their instruments. The commander and his men stood in the doorway.

"You have five minutes, Doctor," barked the Commander. Arturo packed his clothes and toiletries as quick as a flash, stuffing them unevenly in his suitcase. He grew heated and nervous as he packed his things. He felt a pit in his stomach once again, as if he had forgotten something. He prayed to St. Christopher for guidance. He prayed, and he prayed. He clenched his folded hands so tightly that his fingernails left an indentation on the sides. Then a spark flitted his imagination. His eyes opened. In a fit of relief, he turned and saw the picture frame of his family. He took it down and examined it. He stroked

the metal frame with affection. His eyes began to tear up but

were quickly wiped away. Arturo had to do this. He had to do

this for his family. He carefully placed the picture in his

suitcase.

He then turned to the shelf above his bed and opened a

cookie jar. The jar was white, small, and insignificant. It

collected dust and possessed no sweets inside. He reached inside

and picked it up. It was the unholy device. So small, yet so

insignificant. Arturo brought out his handkerchief from his

pocket and dusted it. As the dust sifted away, it began to gleam

in the light. "R.M." was engraved on it in arabesque calligraphy.

Arturo held it tightly in his hands. He closed his eyes. Tears

fought for an escape, but he refused to release them. He heard a

knock on the hut door once again. Arturo stuffed the device in

his breast pocket.

Arturo left with his suitcase, legs shaking slightly as he

was escorted by two soldiers. He winced as he saw their

automatic weapons. They looked familiar and terrifying. They

marched silently despite their size. The only thing that was heard were the black rosary beads that swung back and forth beside their waists. The soldiers escorted Arturo in the second car. Commander Octavian stood beside the opened door of the car and saluted.

"Wait!!!" shouted a distant voice. The soldiers turned, and it was Pino, with a suitcase, running toward the trucks with a trail of all the young children. They all laughed as if playing a game. Their innocent smiles brought a spark of joy to Arturo's heart. Pino had a slight smile on his face as he raced with the children, but his eyes had a look of urgency. The soldiers then pointed their weapons at Pino and the children.

"HALT!!!" shouted one of the soldiers. Pino held up his hands and dropped his suitcase in surrender. The children's smiles disappeared, and they stopped dead in their tracks. The soldiers cocked their weapons and pushed Pino on his knees. He held a small booklet in his hands.

"Commander Octavian, if you will, I wish to join you on your conquest to the witch capital," shouted Pino nervously.

"Pino, what in the blazes are you doing?" Arturo whispered angrily.

The commander chuckled. "Lower your weapons, men. What makes you think we desire to have another Traveler come with us? We do not need another body bag to fill, brother."

"Commander, I promise that I will be of great use. I am a former Samuelite, Giuseppe Alessandro. I was known for helping to end the Slave Uprising of 1910. I was awarded for my efforts."

The commander's eyes widened in surprise. "I thought I recognized you. Your father was a powerful Samuelite captain in Vatican City. You were also that mercenary after your career in Japan and Egypt. I'm shocked to find such a decorated soldier demoted to this squander."

"God has a plan for all of us, Commander. And…I guess He brought me here."

"Very well, you may join us. But the last thing I need is another body bag to fill. First, I must see your credentials."

Pino got up slowly, presented his small booklet, and saluted to Commander Octavian. Commander Octavian read his documents. "Checks out," gruffed the commander. "LET'S MOVE!!!"

Pino then hopped in the vehicle with Arturo. Arturo looked at his brother shockingly as if he were a complete stranger. The engine roared and quickly zoomed, leaving a trail of dust behind their tails. Arturo watched outside his window as the children ran alongside the trucks, waving goodbye to their hero. They blew him kisses, flew the toy airplanes that Arturo had made for them, and sang goodbye songs in their native tongue.

"Goodbye, Doc!"

"Come back soon!"

"Remember us!"

"We love you, Doc!"

Arturo opened his window and waved, smiling bravely at the children. He, for the first time, felt he was doing something right. Arturo felt free and bold. He felt that resurgence that he was doing God's work. Arturo was going to free the people of Africa and all those who suffered. He waved at the smiling children, who were beginning to run too close with the trucks.

BANG! BANG! BANG!

Arturo's smile disappeared. He sat back and glanced blankly at the black emptiness of the truck. His stomach sank, and his heart broke as he heard silent thuds hit the ground of the lifeless African savannah.

4

Arturo and Pino drove for an hour in complete silence.
Both stared out the window as the ominous truck zoomed in at
remarkable speed through the African savannah. Like the view,
their spirits were barren and hopeless. Despite the heat, Arturo
felt cold in his seat. He shivered. He reached into his suitcase
and brought out a blanket. The chief of Johannesburg had given
it to Arturo as a gift. It was green and gold with zig-zag print
embroidered in thick wool. It reminded Arturo of tall grass fields
back in Cassino. He remembered running with his children,
feeling free and young once again. He would chase his children,
carry them, and spin them around in a circle, disappearing in tall
grass. Then the other children would tackle him to release their
captured brother or sister. They would tickle their father and
giggle. What brave little warriors they were. How he missed
them. The blanket was warm, thick, and comfortable. Arturo
snuggled close to it.

Arturo looked at Pino, who was also shivering. Pino looked blank and unfocused. He stared straight ahead of the truck as if envisioning something in his mind. He then shook his head and gave Arturo a little smile, as if he was ready to build yet another house for the village.

"Would you like a blanket, brother?" asked Arturo. "You look freezing."

"Oh no, I'm quite alright, old chap, just slightly tired," said Pino coolly.

"Are you sure? You don't look too sharp."

"I said I am alright, Arturo," said Pino sourly and continued looking out the window. In two years of friendship, Pino had never raised his voice towards Arturo. Pino was always quiet, calm, and optimistic. Arturo had never seen Pino behave this sort of way. Pino's eyes brought a shade of regret and sadness. The poor boy was young and fragile. Arturo sensed something more was bothering him.

"What's really the matter, Pino?" asked Arturo gently. "Is everything quite alright?"

Pino gave him no answer. Arturo looked out the window and sighed. He closed his eyes for a moment. He saw dead acacia trees fallen from the unforgiving winds in the far distance, lying in the desert, turning to rotted dust. He then opened his eyes. Soon, the winds increased speed, picking up dust, making it more difficult to see. In fear, Arturo's eyes closed again. He opened them. His heart began to beat rapidly against his chest as if trying to escape. He began to shake. He couldn't move. He turned to his passengers. Pino and the other soldiers were gone. Instead, Samuelite officers sat beside him, wearing their gray and red uniforms. He recognized a few of their faces. They all sat, heads down, armed to the teeth, and ready for battle. The truck buckled as it sped through the crowded streets. He heard muffled, angry and terrified screams from outside the vehicle. He heard ricocheted gunfire impact the armored car, yet the truck drove on. An officer stood up. He too wore the gray and red uniform but instead featured a golden stripe across his chest plate. It was the captain.

"Alright, men, we are here for one thing and for one thing only: subdue the rioters," barked the captain. "Kill if necessary.

By the glory of God, we shall subdue the enemies of Christ in his holy name. Some of you may die today, but you will die as martyrs under the name of your emperor! Today, you will bring glory to the name of the Church! *Deus vult!*"

"*DEUS VULT!*" shouted the men in unison. Arturo's eyes widened. He remembered this day. He tried to move, but he felt cemented to his seat. He tried to speak, but his lips refused to open. His eyes burned as tears ran down his face. His face turned hot. The truck then abruptly stopped. Arturo internally cried, hot tears streaming down his face. The back doors of the car swung open. An unexpected light blinded the officers momentarily. In a uniformed fashion, the officers rose from their seats. Immediately, Arturo's body shot up from his seat as if being pulled like a marionette. He tried to move his legs and arms, but they were stiff and unwilling. In unison, they put on their helmets. Their helmets covered their faces completely, shielding them entirely. Arturo could hear his shaky breath within the mask. He and his men marched out of the truck. Arturo's eyes widened in immense horror. There stood the burning St. Peter's Basilica.

Slaves of Rome ran in complete chaos, shouting in anger, wearing strange masks, and carrying torches of red flame. Gunshots were fired in every direction; automobiles were flipped over in the streets. Ragged men and women threw torches at the holy building. Windows crashed, and smoke covered the gray, bleak sky. Hate and anger filled the oppressed atmosphere. Thousands of voices wishing to be free were furious like the flames of the holy city. Hundreds of Samuelites fought thousands of rioters. Samuelites shot, clubbed and subdued the rioters. They laughed in the faces of their enemies. One Samuelite pinned a young man onto the ground and slit his throat with a dagger. Another hung a man in a turban on a lamppost. Multiple rioters threw bricks from fallen buildings at the Samuelites. Some daringly painted symbols of their faiths on the walls of the buildings but were ultimately shot down.

The officers raised their shields and firearms towards the crowd. Arturo's arms positioned the submachine gun towards the crowd of furious individuals. Tears streamed from his face. Rioters formed a tight formation, raising their fists in the air.

They held a burning blue flag. They were waving in the wind as they marched. They were unafraid and ready to die.

"*FREEDOM! FREEDOM! FREEDOM!*" shouted the rioters. They all spat and held their fists in a fury.

"OFFICERS HOLD YOUR FORMATION!" shouted the Samuelite captain. The Samuelites formed a tight U-shaped position. "WE FIGHT FOR THE GLORY OF THE EMPEROR! AGAINST THE HERETIC SCUM! FIRE ON MY COMMAND! READY! AIM! FIRE!" Arturo closed his eyes.

***

"Arturo! Arturo! Wake up!" shouted Pino. Arturo opened his eyes and felt a sharp pain on his face. "Are you alright, old boy? You were shouting in your sleep! We tried waking you up, but we couldn't wake you! I even slapped you a few times! Is everything ok? You can talk to me, brother."

"*Benedictus pacis*, my dear brother. I am quite alright, I promise. I just had a bad dream, is all," said Arturo candidly, shaking Pino's hand. Arturo wiped the tears from his eyes and rubbed his swollen cheeks. He could still hear the cries of the innocent from his dream.

"Enough dramatics, Travelers," said Commander Octavian. "We're here at the Cape."

Arturo looked out the window and saw the buzzing city of the Cape. It was white and beautiful, opposite the village of Johannesburg. Flags of the empire waved proudly as speakers from every corner of the broad, black streets played psalms and imperial proclamations on a loop. Shining automobiles zoomed excitedly on the wide roads. Arturo saw thousands of large ships entering and exiting the Cape, bringing exotic spices and minerals to and from Europe. He saw thousands of elites walking among the streets, wearing expensive suits and dresses. He and the other agents got out of their car and explored the grand city.

The smell of coffee immediately wafted toward Arturo's nose. He followed the scent towards a cafe. He saw a couple sitting outside the quaint establishment. The gentleman was of African descent, and he wore a clean cream-colored suit with a red handkerchief on his breast pocket. He had perfect white teeth, golden eyes, and a smooth, youthful face. His wife was of European descent and wore an elegant green dress that complimented her eyes. It was long, silky, and beautiful. She wore a large hat that sprouted peacock feathers atop her head.

The gentleman smiled and took a sip of his espresso cup as his

wife playfully ate her biscuit. Standing beside them was a ragged

man, holding an umbrella over the scorching sun. The young

man looked exhausted as he held the heavy white umbrella. He

was pale, thin, and hungry. He glanced hungrily at his master's

biscuit, wishing he could have a mere crumb. His master

snapped his fingers and he immediately put down the umbrella.

The young man turned his neck. Immediately, Arturo saw the

symbol of the Star of David branded on his neck. He was a

slave.

It had been years since Arturo had smelled the salty

shores of the Atlantic. He felt the sun's warmth tickle his face.

His eyes squinted from the intense African sun. He heard

seagulls squalling over a dead fish by the peer. Arturo and Pino

marched alongside Commander Octavian and HOWs. They

made quite a spectacle of themselves as they marched across the

city's center. The crowded elites moved in reverence of the

soldiers. Like Moses splitting the Red Sea, they parted the crowd with ease. Striking fear to the masses, they moved from their seats.

A statue of a very young Emperor Francesco Bartolomeo stood proudly at its center. The figure was tall, polished, white marble and stood proudly, approximately twenty feet high. It depicted the emperor valiantly holding a sword towards the heavens, while the other had the *Malleus Maleficarum*. Underneath his heels, he stood on the head of a giant serpent. The serpent was made of black marble and crushed under the foot of its mighty papal assailant. The emperor's face expressed pleasantness and strength as if he had no problem slaying a devilish creature underneath his heels. Arturo stood in awe of the prideful masterpiece. He was then pushed by a HOW to continue moving forward. Arturo's ears grew slightly hot in annoyance, but he quickly calmed himself. He patted his pocket in the assurance of the pocket watch's safety. It was secure.

The military party marched down a chasm of one hundred white marble steps. As the steps escalated, a continuous wall-line separated the city from the sea. The wall was massive and pristine. It was as bold as the city. A drop of blood landed on

Pino's shoulder. His eyes widened as he looked up. Two men and a woman hung upside down and naked. Blood dripped from their mouths slowly as flies buzzed around their swollen eyes. Nailed to their genitals were signs that said, "Jew-loving scum," "Muslim Pig," and "Protestant Whore". Pino quickly turned away. His stomach churned, and he felt sick. Arturo looked out and rubbed his wedding band feverishly. Octavian spat on the ground as he looked at the hanging corpses.

"Enemies of the state," Octavian explained. "Serves them right for being traitors of the Holy Father. Probably had their secret meetings. May they rot in fucking hell."

Arturo, Pino, and the soldiers marched down to the docks. Hundreds of cranes heaved enormous crates in and out of their ships. The cranes moaned as they elevated the gigantic metal boxes in the air. The boardwalk creaked as Arturo, and the men marched with heavy boots and armor. It creaked, yet it was stable. On the docks and cargo ships were men wearing nothing but loincloths. They operated the ports, heaving the heavy insides from the metal crates. The boxes were filled with exotic goods and spices. The slaves staggered and grunted as they heaved the precious cargo. Amongst the crowd of slaves, wearing a blue armored uniform, was a slave handler. He stood on a pedestal five feet from the ground, carrying a scourge in his hand. The scourge was long, with a metal hilt and black thongs approximately five feet long. Like a hawk, he patiently waited on his perch to attack his helpless prey.

Amongst the fast-moving crowd, Arturo saw a limping Muslim girl. Her skin was as bright as copper. Her eyes were blood red, mixed with tears and sweat. Her hair was graying, despite her youthful appearance. She was naked, only wearing a loincloth, exposing her bare breasts. The brand on her neck looked fresh. The salt of her sweat burned her with every step she took. Her legs shook vigorously as she attempted to carry the crate that was three times her size. She gasped for air after each step as if she were being suffocated. Arturo noticed that, among the other slaves, she was moving the slowest. The slave handler turned in his perch and watched her closely as she struggled to carry the heavy metal box. Her knees began to wobble. Her blood-stained eyes rolled to the back of her head, and she collapsed. The handler smirked cruelly as if he had been waiting for her to collapse. He brandished his scourge.

"Get up, slave," barked the slave handler, still smirking. Her eyes opened, then closed slightly, clearly distorted, and exhausted.

"She needs food, sir," said an old man with an incredibly long beard, hauling a crate with another young man. "We haven't eaten in days."

"Shut the fuck up, slave!" spat the slaver handler angrily. "Or I'll shove something for her to eat down her fucking throat!"

He then kicked her limp body with his heavy pointed boots, impacting the center of her back. She screamed in agony. Without hesitation, he grabbed her by the ends of her long, graying hair and pulled them above his head. She screamed again. The slaves felt nothing but emptiness in their hearts. Not a spark of hope twinkled in their eyes as they saw their fellow sister being molested by the cruel handler. He then whistled, and two other handlers came. They grabbed her, each taking an arm, and carried her to a tall, bloodied wood post. She kicked and screamed. She cursed at the handlers, demanding to be released. She begged for mercy, yet they showed none. Instead, they laughed. Her tears streamed from her face. Her nose ran. She was helpless. The handler raised his scourge, laughing. His fellow handlers made bets if she would die after ten lashes or twenty. The handler then landed the first strike. Her back immediately tore open, gushing blood. The slave opened her mouth, but no sound escaped. Her eyes bulged in agony. Then a low moan and cry escaped her lips. He then landed another lash. Her cries grew louder and hoarse.

Pino stood in anger at such injustice. His blood boiled with rage. His fists tightened. He felt his heart race and jump within his chest. His feet felt light and ready to pounce. Pino then dropped his suitcase onto the dock. Pino darted past the HOWs and lunged in front of the slave handler, shielding the slave girl. Pino's back was stung with pain. He quickly turned to his combatant and punched the slave handler square in the jaw, immediately knocking him out.

The other two handlers looked at their fallen friend in awe. The first one was tall. He swung for a blow, but Pino immediately ducked and punched the handler on the side of his leg, making him kneel. Pino then punched him on the side of the head, knocking him out cold. The second handler was larger and stockier in build, so tall he cast a large shadow over Pino. He looked down at his fallen brother. The lanky veteran punched him straight in the stomach, but the handler barely flinched. He merely laughed and punched Pino square in the gut. Pino then fell to the ground. Pino attempted to stand and looked up at the giant, but the giant kicked him on his left cheek. Pino felt the metal boot of the handler meet his soft, chiseled cheek. A shock of pain spread throughout his face. Blood poured from his lips. A new cut was opened, leaving a small trail of blood. Pino felt the warmth reach his chin. He tasted the blood. It tasted foul and metallic as if Pino were holding nails between his teeth, as he did when he built houses for the people of Johannesburg. Pino felt empty and helpless as he lay on the dock in excruciating pain.

The young slave then sobbed beside Pino as she wiped his blood with her own hair on the wooden dock. She then shielded him as the giant handler lifted his scourge above his head, ready to strike.

55

"HALT!" shouted a familiar muffled voice. It was Commander Octavian. He and his men surrounded the giant handler as he stood over the fallen Pino. "Stand down, handler! How dare you stand away from your post," the commander said as he marched toward the scene. He pointed at his men to lift the fallen Pino. Blood trickled from his lips.

"It was the Traveler scum, comrade," declared the handler. "He had no right to be wallowing about on *my* dock."

"Is that so?" the commander said, surprised. Without hesitation, he slapped the slave handler with the back of his hand. The handler glared at the commander with wild eyes.

"I think you forgot your place, handler," continued Octavian. "I would suggest that you and your men learn to better handle your slaves. Will you do this?"

Immediately, the giant handler knelt to the commander in false contrition. His eyes closed in annoyance, knowing the ranking of his superior. "Yes, my commander," gritted the handler.

"Your duty is to ensure that there is no insurrection amongst the slaves. You are to maintain peace and ensure that these dogs and enemies of the empire are put in their place and realize the might of our Lord and Emperor. You are to teach them the ways of our Lord and make them beg for forgiveness, correct?"

"Yes, my commander."

"Instead, you flog the greatest warrior of our empire. A punishment such as that could be considered treason. Are you a traitor, handler?"

"No, commander!" The handler then stood in salute to his superior. "I love my empire and my emperor! I will die for the glory of God and his disciples. I am a proud citizen, my lord. Please accept my act of contrition, my commander."

Commander Octavian grinned, pleased with the handler's cowardice. Octavian then walked to the slave girl. His boots thumped the boardwalk with each step. The slave closed her eyes and cowered in fear. He chuckled. He gently lifted her chin as she sobbed silently. Tears streamed down her sunken cheeks. He then hushed her and wiped her tears. As if in slow motion, he grabbed a full head of her hair. With a blink of an eye, he brandished his knife and slit her throat. Her cries turned into gurgles, and she collapsed. He then cleaned his knife with her hair.

"Show us to our ship, the *Archangel*, handler," coolly demanded the commander. "Also, do clean up this mess. There is blood on your dock."

5

Smoke filled the blood-red sky. Torches and buildings blazed in horrendous flame. The air was angry, violent, and heavy. One could smell the stench of death as the Samuelite soldiers massacred the rebels. Arturo trembled within his boots as he held his weapon towards the enemy. He watched in horror as St. Peter's Basilica's roof collapsed. Hundreds of years of architecture were destroyed within seconds. The house of God crumbled before his very eyes.

A man with blonde curly hair and wild eyes emerged from the smoke. He stood on a column of rubble, wearing nothing but a chest plate and a Samuelite helmet painted red. He had a long beard that was dyed blue. He waved a flag in one hand while wielding an ax with another, urging his comrades to continue their battle. He made eye contact with Arturo. His wild eyes were animalistic and hungry. He plunged his flag into the rubble. It stood waving in hopeful triumph. He jumped down *from the column of debris with an ample grunt. He gave a few*

deep breaths and growled, then gave an incredible yawp. Arturo

froze. The screaming barbarian ran towards him. Arturo's

fighting instincts gave in, and he aimed his weapon at the rebel.

"Take the shot, soldier," barked the captain behind him,

taking off his helmet. "Take the fucking—"

***

Arturo then felt a hand shake his shoulder. Arturo closed

his eyes tightly and then opened them. He was sitting in the

infirmary. He had fallen asleep as he sat beside Pino. Pino was

heavily bandaged, lying in a cot, his arm in a sling. He smiled at

Arturo calmly.

"The doctors thought we lost you too, old sport," Pino

said in a raspy but cheerful tone. "It's a miracle that you're

awake."

"Well, it's a miracle you're even alive, brother," said

Arturo smartly. "What did the medic say?"

"The usual. Concussion. Bruised ribs. Bruised jaw. Nothing too fancy, old chap. It's not my first rodeo getting wounds like these. At least my face still looks pretty."

Arturo laughed. He then got up, poured himself a glass of water, and handed it to Pino, who sipped it carefully. His arms shook slightly as he held the glass of water. Pino winced in pain, but he tried his best to remain strong for his brother. He took a sip, smacked his lips, and smiled at his friend. Arturo shook his head.

"Still, that was very stupid what you did," said Arturo concerningly. His tone was almost fatherly as if telling one of his boys to stop teasing their younger siblings.

"I know, Arturo. But remember that raid we had to break up back in Johannesburg?"

"Dear God, how could I forget! Seven Dutchmen and three Namibians. Those rascals were hard to negotiate. We really had to give an arm and a leg for water supplies. Good God were they armed! What was it that they carried with them?"

"Five machine guns, two grenade launchers, and an Inquisition tank armed to the teeth! Clearly black market! I wonder how the hell those Dutchmen got their hands on such a beauty! I mean, she was really massive! Reminds me of the good old days."

"Well, brother, I wouldn't say the 'good' old days," said Arturo candidly. "Do remember your vows. I think the doctor gave you a bit too many pain pills."

"I am fine! No need to baby me, you nancy boy! I am completely fine. But you're quite right, brother. You're quite right." Silence lingered in the air for a while. The room was stagnant, sanitized, and bleak. Pino then broke the silence. "You know there are some days I actually miss it."

"You miss what, Pino?"

"I miss *it*. Being in the shit! I actually miss holding a rifle sometimes. Life was so much simpler. We were just told what to do, pray, and not worry about anything. Not really much the same as what we do now."

"Are you saying that what we do now is not good?"

"No, brother, of course not!"

"Then why do you still miss 'the good old days?'"

Pino's face turned slightly red in annoyance. "It's because I actually felt like we were doing something," Pino said hotly but tried to remain calm and composed. "We were actually making a difference within the world. I felt like we were shaping our world into something extraordinary."

"Yes, but we made a difference by killing people. Massacring and conquering innocent lives! Many did not deserve to die! You know that! Innocent lives are being thrown away like the coins of our chapels. Think about that poor slave girl."

"Arturo, you are completely wrong. We did nothing to save her! It was our vows that killed her!"

Arturo's ears grew hot. "Pino, this is blasphemy! We took vows to bring peace, just as Christ did. We vow not to fight. We bring peace and hope to the misfortunate. Pacifism is the way. The Inquisition is nothing but a congregation of hypocrites!

What the Inquisition promotes is not the work of Christ! If anything, it is the work of the Devil himself! We are no better than the Americans, Pino!"

"Arturo, you do not know what you are talking about! We are nothing but fools! I had to do something to save that poor girl! Arturo, you saw what they were doing to that slave girl! She deserved j--"

"Brother, please be quiet! They are already listening to us."

Pino's pain was rising, and his head grew slightly dizzy. He took a sip of his water. He took a deep breath and whispered, "Justice, Arturo. She deserved justice." He then sighed in defeat. Arturo looked at his feet in thought. The girl did deserve justice. His job as a Traveler was to bring hope for all he came across, and he had failed. Like the girl, Arturo felt hopeless.

"You are right, my dear brother," Arturo said quietly. "Today, we failed. We both failed and broke our vows today. You acted, and I did nothing to help her. I was nothing but a selfish fool that only cared for my safety. I am so sorry, brother.

I do worry about this mission."

Pino removed his bandaged arm from his sling and
patted Arturo's shoulder. "It's going to be alright, old chap. We
must remember *Benedictus pacis*."

"That is right. *Benedictus—*"

A soldier then busted the door open. "Dr. Mattei, Mr.
Alessandro. You are requested on the bridge."

Arturo got up from his chair. He patted his pocket to
ensure that the watch was still in his keeping. His eyes widened.
He urgently dug his hand in all his pockets. The device was not
there. The watch was gone.

***

The *Archangel* hummed softly as Arturo, Pino, and the
squadron of naval officers escorted them down the narrow
corridor. As they marched, Arturo couldn't help but observe the
aquatic titanium tube. He saw the sub's age. It had an old-
fashioned exterior and handiwork. The rusty bucket was not

modern, like the ones he had seen before he left Europe to be a Traveler. All the models made today were poorly made compared to models he had seen in the past. Pino seemed unnerved by the situation. Arturo was slightly relieved but concerned at the same time. He felt naked without his watch. He felt vulnerable and terrified. He had to know where it was and who had stolen it from him. The bridge gate opened.

On the bridge, fifty naval officers controlled the deck. There was a slight murmur amongst the men. Each man sat on a metal desk, where a radar, telephone, and a frantic, yet disciplined officer sat ready for his next task. A phone rang every few seconds as messages were exchanged from the sea to the mainland. A highly decorated gentleman stood in the center of the room, looking out to a vast window that opened to the entire room. He stood proudly with his hands and feet in relaxed attention. He was confident and bold. Commander Octavian stood below him, also observing the window. Arturo could see the vast blue sea as they zoomed through the highly pressured waters, hundreds of feet below the surface. He then looked out the window in awe. It had been years since he had been in a sub.

Arturo then saw a large bronze plaque that hung proudly beside the window. It was illuminated by two small lights. The plaque read:

THE ARCHANGEL

EST. 1891

MANUFACTURED BY THE MATTEI FAMILY GUILD

Arturo frowned in shame. The *Archangel* was created by his kin. Given its age, Arturo knew that the Church realized that all their current weapons and military vehicles had been absolutely useless. Only the Mattei family had created such perfect instruments of death. The Church had been unable to mimic the beauty of such intelligent design. All inventors have tried and failed. Arturo was the last of a proud line of inventors. He was the last of a group of remarkable people that revolutionized the modern world. Now, he was off to the most dangerous continent in the world.

"Show a leg, boys! We have 0800 hours until we reach the Devil's shit." The old officer turned and smiled at Arturo. "Remarkable, isn't it? One of the finest submarines the Inquisition has ever seen and built by the finest engineers. Built by the Mattei Family Guild, it was," stated the old officer. His voice was gruff yet endearing. Arturo felt his honorable presence. He seemed like a man of sensibility and honor.

"I have never been on a sub as big as this one," said Arturo in awe.

"Well, if you're a sea dog as old as me, size never matters," chortled the captain. "The name is Captain John Thaler II. But they all call me Blackjack. I'm the commanding officer of this old duck. Who might you be, young man?"

"My name is Dr. Arturo Mattei. A pleasure to meet you, Captain." Arturo reached out and shook the captain's hand firmly.

"Well, I'll be damned! I never thought I'd see the day when I'd meet another Mattei! Your family has done incredible work, young man. You should be proud!"

"Thank you, Captain," said Arturo awkwardly. The subject of his family was always an awkward one.

"In fact, it was your father that built the *Archangel*! Your father was a great, great man. I knew him for about 30 years!"

Blackjack reached into his pocket and pulled out an old, tattered leather wallet. He took a small black and white photograph from his wallet and handed it to Arturo. Arturo smiled to himself for the first time since he had left Johannesburg. In the picture, he saw his father, a tall, slender man with a mustache, much like his, standing stiffly next to a much younger Blackjack. He, too, wore a uniform. They both didn't smile in the photo. Both men looked very distinguished and powerful. In his father's hand, he held a cigarette. Behind him was the brand new, freshly painted *Archangel*. Arturo turned the photograph, and a short message was scrawled in the back. It read:

KEEP YOUR HEAD ABOVE THE WATER, BLACKJACK
    SINCERELY,
    ROBERTO MATTEI, HONG KONG 1891

Arturo smiled to himself and handed the photo back to Blackjack.

"Your father was a great man, Doc. He really was. I can't remember the last time I met a man as incredible as him. He had a brilliant mind, he did. His mind was like a clock. Calculated and precise. He knew who to trust. Times like these, you gotta be careful."

"Indeed," responded Arturo quietly.

"Your brother, Junior, was another great man. Never met a finer soldier in the entire Inquisition. I've been around a long time and have never met someone as brave as your brother."

"Indeed, he was, Captain. He really was."

"I remember meeting him in Jerusalem!"

"You've met Roberto in Jerusalem?"

"Why yes! I remember being in the market, and some scallywag was trying to bum him off a broken watch! He still bought the damn thing. I bought one myself! At least mine worked!" The old captain then brandished a watch almost identical to Arturo's. Same design, same shape, only a different purpose. This watch ticked with life.

"I remember him talking about you," Blackjack continued. "He wanted to give you that watch. He always cared about his fellow soldiers. That was the last time I ever saw him. What a shame. A damn shit storm the Chesapeake mission was."

Arturo was silent for a moment. Blackjack realized that he had said too much. He pursed his lips and patted Arturo's back.

"I am sorry, Doc. Sometimes once you get me talking, I never shut the hell up."

"It's quite alright, Captain. I did my duty as a soldier of the Church and Christ. That part of my life is behind me, and now I serve God. Today, I serve my Church."

Blackjack smiled. "*Benedictus pacis*," he responded softly, giving Arturo a slight wink. Arturo was shocked for a moment and gave a small sigh of relief. He had another person to trust.

"Captain," barked Commander Octavian. "Would you mind walking Dr. Mattei and Mr. Alessandro through our plan of action?"

"Aye, aye, Commander," militantly responded Blackjack. Arturo saw the captain's kindness wash away completely. It was as if he was putting on a mask. The kind Captain Blackjack had left the room. Captain Thaler was on deck.

"Gentlemen, we are now approximately 200 miles away from our destination. We must discuss our plan of attack."

He looked at his watch and then pressed a button. A large metal table descended from the ceiling. It revealed a blank screen. Lieutenants and officers of various ranks surrounded the table. Blackjack then pointed to his quartermaster. The quartermaster immediately pressed a few buttons on the side of the table, and a hologram of a world map appeared.

"Mr. Grosso, move to our current location."

"Yes, Captain," responded the officer quickly.

The image moved to a small image of the *Archangel*. There they saw it as it was closely approaching the mysterious forbidden continent. The continent of North America looked vast and dangerous.

"Gentlemen, I present to you the Devil's Playground. Thousands and thousands of miles of wilderness and unknown territory," said Blackjack gruffly. "However, we have received only some information on the Devil's Playground. A few hundred years ago, our former Puritan brothers and sisters claimed the northern territory as their own and blessed it as a new haven in the name of God. However, this new Eden was defiled by the followers of Satan. Like rats, they went onto their ships and spread their disease in an English colony of what was known as Massachusetts. Hundreds of cases of this plague spread from town to town. The leaders of this town wanted to fight the grasp of Satan by every means necessary. They imprisoned and rightfully executed witches.

It wasn't until October 30, 1692, in a small bum-fuck town called Salem, the witches had enough. Under the command of their hag priestesses, they slaughtered all the children of Salem in the dead of night. Soon, other witches from other towns began slaughtering their children. This slaughter then spread to the South, where our Spanish brothers and sisters resided. The colonists then fled back to Europe and begged the Inquisition to help cleanse their lands. The Inquisition then usurped the Vatican, and we have been at war since. It has been hundreds of years since Christians have successfully touched the continent. Now it is under the hands of Satan and its followers. We have tried and failed. But today, the *Archangel* will breach the forbidden land. And like the Hand of God, we will strike upon the witches!"

"DEUS VULT!" shouted the officers around the table.

"This will be Operation Haxan, gentlemen," continued Blackjack. "The *Archangel* will advance onto Salem Harbor ten miles east. Then we will anchor and send our mini-subs, our darts, to launch an attack on the enemy. We must be careful of any enemy attacks. We may have the best of the best, gentlemen, but the enemy has some technology as well. We need to watch for Indig subs. The Indigenous American Confederation has been allied with the witches for a few hundred years and they are just as lean and mean as the rest of them. We may lose a few darts, boys. But, by God, we will give them hell. We will land our darts north of the Harbor, someplace where the enemy is not patrolling their shores. Commander Octavian, I leave the ground plan to you."

The commander stepped forward. "We will send our HOW units to scout and inspect the area," said Commander Octavian. "If the coast is clear, we will set up camp one hundred kilometers north from the main city. We do not know much about the cartography of this area because our drones were taken down by the enemy."

"So, we are basically walking in there blind?" asked Pino, astonished.

"Yes, we are, Officer Alessandro," glared the commander.

"This is a goddamn suicide mission! How the hell are we supposed to know where to go? We know nothing about the land

and how many enemy civilians are surrounding the area! If we don't know anything about the land and the enemy, we might as well put a bullet in our skulls right this second!"

"He's right," chimed Arturo. Arturo felt a lodge in his throat. The officers around the room spoke amongst each other softly. "Yes, there are lots of trees and wilderness, but that doesn't mean that there are still people in those woods. I have been on a mission like this, and I have to say it's suicide. The last mission the Inquisition sent us to, I was there. I went to the Chesapeake and saw how the enemy operated. The witches were part of the woods. They hung to the branches like birds and slaughtered my squad. They slaughtered my brother. And that was just in the Carolinas. We are entering the very belly of the beast, gentlemen. We are talking about the very capital of the Devil's Playground. We need to have eyes on the back of our heads!"

Commander Octavian looked somewhat surprised. Blackjack gave a small smile to Arturo but quickly wiped it away before the Commander saw it. Diplomacy was never

Arturo's most vital skill. He recalled his father making him rehearse for hours on end speeches that he would say on behalf of his father in various international meetings and ceremonies.

"Very rational, Dr. Mattei," growled Octavian. "Yes, it is a suicide mission. Yes, we are going in blind. However, you are under the protection of the Hammer of Witches. That is why you are here, Doctor. Gentlemen, may I present to you the answer. Mr. Grosso, if you will."

The officer then pressed a button, and an image of the watch appeared before them. Arturo's eyes widened. Pino looked at Arturo with immense shock. Commander Octavian smirked.

"Dr. Arturo Mattei here is one of the most brilliant minds in modern times. He is the last surviving member of the Mattei Family Guild. Dr. Mattei has invented the answer on how to win this war, in honor of his Emperor, Church, and all the lives that have been lost under the hands of the enemy."

"Do tell me, Doc," asked the Captain uncomfortably. "What does this device do?"

Arturo then took a deep breath.

"It's a hammer, Captain. It is the Hammer of God."

6

All the naval officers and military leaders muttered amongst themselves in awe and fear. Arturo felt nothing but shame and discomfort.

"This weapon is what will bring total annihilation to the enemy," Arturo continued. "Imagine the greatest hellfire meeting the might of God. The Hammer will decimate hundreds upon hundreds of miles, taking any living thing straight to hell with it. It requires one of the most unholy means of power. It is a damn miracle that such a device of that size holds much power. If Death wished to replace His weapon, he would only need this pocket watch."

"And if we want to detonate this device, we will need proper ground control," declared Pino. "I volunteer to lead our ground patrol to ensure this mission goes smoothly and safely. Mind you, some of us do have families to go to."

Pino then looked at Arturo in reassurance, and Arturo nodded in thanks.

"Granted," said Octavian. "You will help lead our fellow HOWs on foot to secure the area. We will camp twenty miles north of the center of Salem. Then we will go into the center of the city incognito and detonate the Hammer. Only Dr. Mattei knows the combination of this weapon. We must ensure the highest security for it."

"Commander, where is the device at the moment?" asked Blackjack.

"At the moment, the Hammer is under the high security of the HOWs. It is securely kept within this ship, and no further questions will be asked of its whereabouts."

"Very well! Meeting adjourned! Back to your stations, you dogs! We will arrive at 0800 hours."

The men then saluted to their captain and returned to their original positions. Arturo stared at the projection of his vile invention. Feelings of regret overwhelmed him. Not only had he lost his device, but he had lost all hope of seeing his family again. Everything seemed absolutely hopeless now.

***

Arturo and Pino were then escorted into their rooms. The door was locked behind them. Arturo and Pino both sat in their beds in silence.

"What in God's name are we going to do now, Pino?" whispered Arturo.

"We have to fight, brother," Pino whispered back. "We have to get the hell out of here. We are going to die for nothing tomorrow! We might as well put a bullet in our mouth and get it over with!"

"I agree, Pino. But they have the device! Those mongrels took it while I was sleeping! We need to get it back."

"How do you suppose we're supposed to do that? We will be reaching America in a few hours. Plus, there is a guard outside of the door!"

Arturo thought long and hard. He stroked his mustache. He heard the hum of the submarine. He looked out the porthole and saw the complete darkness of the sea. It was mysterious, eerie, and unpredictable. Arturo then fidgeted with his wedding band, praying for an idea. Then his wedding band slipped off his finger and rolled underneath the door. He then looked at Pino. He sparked an idea.

Pino hid behind the door with one of the pillows in his hand, ready for the attack. Arturo then took a deep breath and knocked on the door. A burly naval officer gruffed and opened it. He was tall, stupid-looking, and carried an electric cattle prod at his side.

"What do you want?" barked the guard. "All soldiers and personnel are required to be asleep at this time."

"I am sorry to bother you, sir, but it appears that I have dropped my wedding band under the door. Would it be possible for you to grab it for me?"

The guard sighed in annoyance. He then looked onto the ground and saw the shiny gold wedding band. He then huffed in annoyance to bend over. He picked it up and handed it over to Arturo.

"Thank you, good sir!" Arturo said in his most friendly and priestly voice. "That is very kind of you to do that for us holy men. I hate to be a huge bother, but would it be possible for you to check and see if there are any rats in this room? My brother and I were sleeping, and we swore that we heard a scurrying of some sort."

"And why should I give a shit about rats?"

"Well, I can tell that you are an honorable man of your station, sir. According to the Inquisitional Navy's handbook, every sailor and/or officer is responsible for the health and wellness of not only the ship but also the crew. Now, we don't want any potential illnesses and diseases to be spread onto the ship, don't you, sir? Rodents do bring disease. Not to mention, I am an essential individual that is instrumental in this ship's mission. I wouldn't want to catch any diseases and die before starting the mission. That would be awfully foolish on your part because you would be solely responsible for...."

"Shut the fuck up! I'll check your room. Move out of the way."

The guard then trudged through the room and started tossing the bed and pillows. Pino then quickly slammed the door shut.

"What the hell," shouted the guard. "You can't—"

Then Pino and Arturo climbed on top of him and tackled him, putting the pillows over his face. Arturo heard the muffled grunts and screams. The guard was strong. He slammed into the walls and knocked over the lamp. Thankfully, the walls were completely soundproof. The entire ship could never hear the brawl in the tiny room. After five minutes, the guard's movements became slower and slower. He then finally collapsed on top of the bed. Arturo and Pino looked at the fallen guard.

"Oh dear God, did we kill him," asked Arturo, concerned.

Pino checked the guard's pulse. "No, he's passed out cold."

"Quick! Put on his uniform!"

"Why?"

"That way, you can pretend that you are a guard escorting me around the sub. That way, we don't raise suspicion."

"Good plan, brother. *Benedictus pacis.*"

"*Benedictus pacis*, brother."

Pino quickly switched his clothes and put on the guard's uniform. Thankfully, Pino was around the same height as the guard. Pino strapped the electric cattle prod to his side. Playing his disguise brilliantly, Pino grabbed Arturo roughly by the shoulder and escorted him out of the room. They passed a few armed officers. Arturo could hear the hum of the submarine echo through the narrow hallways. From a distance, they saw Commander Octavian marching to his dormitory.

They silently waited until the hallway was clear and tiptoed toward Octavian's dormitory. Arturo and Pino silently opened the door with just a simple crack. They saw Octavian sitting in the middle of the floor, completely naked. His scarred, nude body was illuminated by candlelight.

He held an old red candle in his hand that was lit. He was also surrounded by other small black candles. He then let go of the red candle, and it began to float! He levitated his hand over the flame. His flesh sizzled and produced a stem of smoke. Octavian whispered strange words as he held the candle. He then brandished Arturo's watch and held it to his heart. His eyes rolled onto the back of his head. Arturo and Pino stood silently in awe and in horror.

"Oh my God, Pino," whispered Arturo. "The commander is a witch!"

Pino was about to respond to their discovery. Then the sirens of the *Archangel* blared, and a red light flashed around them.

7

Arturo and Pino fell into a brief state of panic as the red lights flashed and the alarm blared. Sailors and crewmembers scrambled throughout the submarine hallways. Constant clacks of boots and wide-eyed sailors ran in every direction. Octavian, now fully dressed, opened his door in a great state of panic. He glared at Arturo with his gray steel eyes.

"Private, what in God's name is the asset doing out of his dormitory?"

Pino, bewildered that Octavian failed to recognize him, stood at attention. "The asset wished to speak to you, sir," said Pino gruffly, trying his very best to disguise his voice. Thankfully his mask covered his face.

"Well, it's too late. We're under attack! The asset must personally stay with me. Dr. Mattei, come with me."

"Where will I be going, Commander?" asked Arturo nervously.

"We need to get to the darts immediately. We need to move. NOW!"

Arturo nodded. He and Pino then followed Commander Octavian. Although the commander's face was covered, Arturo could see the state of panic in his eyes. He saw the commander in a new light. He saw despite his strong armored exterior; he was weak and alert. The commander was a cold and calculated man, after all. He was secretive and crude. He sought answers in any way necessary. He was meant to represent the most loyal lapdogs of the Inquisition. But after seeing him stripped from his armor, Arturo saw who he truly was…a witch.

Arturo, Pino, and the commander quickly paced towards the main deck. Blackjack stood as he ensured all personnel to leave the main deck and head to the escape pods. Commander Octavian saluted the captain, but the captain did not return a salute. Blackjack was red in the face. He scratched his neatly trimmed beard nervously as his eye twitched and ticked. The red light continued to flare.

"Captain, who's attacking the sub?" asked Commander Octavian.

"Indig subs. They're fighting mad," said the captain.

"Good God, man. Are we not going to fight?"

"There is no chance, Octavian. This old girl is not going to make it. Approximately fifteen Indigs are on our tail. We are toast."

"Captain, there is no way in hell we are going to allow these fucking reds to shoot us down! We are warriors of Christ, Captain! We need to fight the enemy! Tell your men to fire at will!"

"Commander, with all due respect, fightin' in the sea' is not the same as fightin' on land. I believe in God and want to preserve His name, Commander, but I also want to preserve the name of my sailors. This mission is an utter failure. We were doomed from the start."

"Pull yourself together, Captain! All hope is not lost! We have the key to winning this war right here." The commander then pointed at Arturo. Blackjack looked at Arturo with sunken eyes. His eyes were lost as if looking for a light at the end of a dark tunnel. He then gazed upon Arturo for a moment and smiled. He then gave Arturo a wink.

"You know what, Commander. You are absolutely right. We do have the key to winning this war. He stands before me in all his power. We are standing in the presence of greatness, Commander. We are standing with what may be the answer to all my prayers. With that, my commander, I say go to hell."

He then turned and punched Commander Octavian square on this side of his temple. Arturo and Pino stood as if their feet had been cemented. The commander rose and tackled Blackjack. They punched and kicked and clawed each other like wild animals. Blackjack pulled out his pistol and shot a few rounds, but the commander blocked him. They wrestled and brawled as they tried to dominate and kill one another. The commander then flipped Blackjack onto his stomach and grabbed him by the scruff of his beard. Iwas covered in blood. Octavian looked directly at Arturo, brandished his knife, and slit Blackjack's throat. His piercing grey eyes crinkled in a devious smile. He cleaned his bloodied knife with the side of his leg. The red lights and alarms continued to blare and flash.

"I think this is goodbye, Dr. Mattei. All I need from you is this device." He then reached into his pocket and brandished the watch tauntingly. "I believe that you are no longer of use to me. We're going to win this war, Doctor, with or without you. We are finally going to win it! Blood will rain upon the world in a fiery fury at last! Farewell, Doctor. Farewell."

The commander then left the room. Alarms still blared as distant yells and screams of fear were heard outside. Arturo and Pino ran to the fallen Blackjack. Blood pooled onto the floor. Arturo could hear the old captain desperately gasping for air. His eyes widened in shock.

"Oh, Christ! He's bleeding out," Pino said sourly. Pino then threw his helmet across the room. He covered Blackjack's wound, trying his best to close it to stop the bleeding. The captain continued gasping, holding Arturo's hand tightly. A single tear ran across his cheek. With all his strength, he reached down from his pocket and pulled out a pocket watch. No, it wasn't just any old pocket watch. Blackjack clicked the top of the watch. The case popped open only to reveal the head of the case. The watch was dead silent. It was the unholy device.

Arturo gasped. The Commander had taken the decoy. Blackjack pulled Arturo by the collar and said in Arturo's ear almost in a whisper, "Keep your head…above…the water, Arturo…Keep your…head…above…the…." Blackjack's eyes looked towards the watch, then at Arturo, and pointed at Roberto's engraving. His eyes bulged and he took a long breath. Captain Blackjack was dead.

Arturo felt numb once more.

"Arturo, we need to go to the escape pods! We must act now, brother!" said Pino frantically. "We need to move now!"

They ran down the corridor and saw a row of darts with sailors and military personnel entering them as they were ready to be launched. Men were shouting orders and commands.

Young privates were scrambling to ensure that they had all the supplies needed. All the men went to their respective pods. Luckily enough, pods were available to all the crew even if one failed to eject from the sub. This was another graceful genius of the Mattei family. The red lights and horn continued to flash, blinding Arturo. Arturo felt the *Archangel* shake. Arturo looked out the porthole and saw approximately 15 enemy subs approaching the ship and releasing hell. Time was running out!

Arturo and Pino went inside an unoccupied dart. The dart was quaint, circular, but spacious for the two of them. Six bunks stood at its sides, and the controls stood straight away. A window of black separated them from the incalculable dangers of the enemy and the unknown vastness of the sea. Immediately Arturo and Pino jumped to the control panel.

"Do you know how to drive this thing?" Pino said, trying his best to remain calm. A boom on the side of the ship could be heard. The pod shook and tossed. The *Archangel* had been hit! They had to move fast!

"Good Lord, this is ancient. Yes, I think I can. It'll be like riding a motorbike, but I think I can manage." Another boom, and the sub shook furiously. Arturo then said a silent prayer to himself and started the dart. The old bucket then whooshed out like a bullet.

"Praise God!" shouted Arturo, lifting his hands in the air. Soon, a red light flashed on the control screen. The screen read,

POD FUEL: LOW / 20 MILES

"Pino, please give me the coordinates! Someplace remote because we are running low on fuel."

"Here, go to 42°31'57.3"N 70°47'16.7"W," Pino said, looking at the small screen that showed a bird's eye view of a small landmass. "It's a small island off of Massachusetts. I think it will be safe there. It looks habitable. There seems to be no mainland for miles."

"Perfect, we will head there. *Benedictus pacis*, my dear brother."

The dart quickly zoomed away from the remnants of *Archangel*. The old submarine sank to the very depths of Davy Jones's locker. Arturo witnessed various other darts being decimated by the enemy fighter subs in the distance. With furious anger, they zoomed and shot at the enemy darts. The duo saw a small fleet of enemy darts that darted toward the *Archangel* at full force, completely destroying it, killing the darts instantly. Arturo and Pino witnessed the slaughter as they ignited the dark depths of the deep like fireworks. The Travelers bid the fallen a silent prayer of grief and continued their journey to enemy territory. They were headed to America.

8

The night was alive and mysterious. A thick and ominous fog engulfed the island whole. A full moon hid behind the graying sky, unable to pierce the uninhabited island with its light. The sound of crickets and the eerie wind loomed. A few trees sprouted across the island, and its branches blew into the wind. The branches sang and moaned into the night. The tall grasses tickled and danced with life. Arturo and Pino landed their dying vessel onto the island's beach. The sand felt soft, delicate, and untouched. Arturo and Pino knelt in exhaustion and prayed in relief. However, Arturo felt a pit in his stomach, knowing of the great dangers beyond the gray mist.

Pino opened his safety bag. It carried all the necessary items for survival: a fire-starter, an ax, a pistol, a metal pot, a spoon, a water purifier, two weeks' worth of non-perishable food, a torch, a whistle, and a medical kit. Arturo got his ax and began chopping down a nearby tree. He gathered a few logs, some sticks, and dry leaves. He tore a piece of his shirt and tied the bundle together. He then ignited his fire starter. Immediately the flame ignited. The little spark of flame jumped and tried to bite Arturo. Then he picked it up, and the flame grew smaller, cowering in fear but still devouring its leafy meal. Arturo then set the tiny little flame in the middle of a teepee-shaped pile of wood. He blew on the little flame, feeding it oxygen. The flame started to smoke and grow larger and larger. Arturo and Pino began preparing their meal next to a roaring bonfire within minutes. They were pleased with their new, warm hearth.

"You always had a knack for fires, old boy," said Pino in a soft yet cheery tone.

"I love starting fires," chuckled Arturo. "I grew up around fires. Boy, I remember my old man sent me to this old, old, old tinker named Massimo. Mind you, I never knew if he was family or not, but he felt like an uncle in some way or another."

"How old were you?"

"I was only six years old and barely able to reach over the anvils. I remember having to start fires so young. I remember how Massimo would make me chop these large wooden logs twice my size. The logs would give me splinters because he made me carry them and set them in the fire. Starting the fire was my favorite part! Soon I started setting fire to everything! I almost blew up my damn bedroom!"

"No kidding! I never pictured you as the troublesome type."

"Oh, trust me, being taught how to tinker at six was one of my family's greatest achievements, but also their greatest mistake! My poor mother would fear that I would burn Cassino to the ground! But my father would simply laugh. Then he would yell at Roberto to try and build his aeroplane."

Arturo grew quiet for a moment, and the fire began to crackle. "Was Roberto a lot like you?" asked Pino.

"No, he was quite the opposite," continued Arturo. "He wanted to be a soldier, not an inventor like my family wanted him to be. I remember I would sneak into his room late at night, and he would tell me stories of amazing heroes of old. He would tell the stories of Samson, King David, and all those remarkable heroes. Roberto was always the one putting out the flames that I would start! I remember when we would make rockets and try to shoot them at the priest's window! By God, my father was furious. Thankfully, Father was the important person he was. Otherwise, we would've gotten a worse punishment. Roberto would say that he was the one who shot the rocket at the priest's window. Roberto took a lot of hits for me. He was a good brother."

There was silence for a moment.

"But do tell me, brother," asked Arturo candidly, changing the subject. "What made you want to be a Samuelite?"

"I wanted to be like my old man. When I was 16, I was stationed in Tokyo. God, I hated my job. I remember having to arrest so many innocent people for the most ridiculous reasons. I remember one time, I had to crash a Jewish wedding! Imagine fifty people in a cramped basement. Arrested the whole wedding party, we did. I remember enjoying it. I really, really did. Later, I retired from the force, did some mercenary work in Namibia and Egypt, and then became a Traveler."

"Who was your father, Pino? Because I remember Octavian said that he was a well-known captain for the Samuelite forces."

"Well, my father was a captain in Vatican City. His name was Captain Sergio Alessandro."

Arturo's jaw dropped. "You won't believe me, old boy. But I worked with your father."

"Wait, Arturo, you were a Samuelite?" asked Pino completely astounded.

"Yes, I was. After my mission in the Chesapeake, I wanted to honor my brother and continue his legacy as a soldier. I then asked the Archbishop of Cassino for his permission to promote me to join the Samuelite police force. He proudly accepted, much to my parents' disapproval. I actually fought with your father at the Slave Uprising of 1910 in St. Peter's Basilica."

"I'll be damned! I never knew you were a Samuelite!"

"Yes, I was a Samuelite for a few years. I remember that day as if it were yesterday."

Arturo looked at the fire nervously. He felt Pino looking at him. Studying him. "That's what you have been dreaming about, haven't you? All those nightmares?" asked Pino quietly. The wind blew towards them directly, and a wave of coolness and heat brushed their faces.

"I just remember those people, Pino. I just remember seeing all that fire. All that blood. I felt so responsible for it all. I felt that I was only creating a bigger problem. All those people. All those poor souls. They're all dead. Slaves and Samuelites. I was a murderer, brother. Yet, I am still here. The very Devil himself has me on his very palm! I couldn't put out the fires, Pino! I couldn't put out those fires."

"Arturo, you are speaking absolute nonsense! You are not a murderer! You are a good man! You sacrificed yourself to travel millions of miles away from home, away from your family, to help the children of God! You are not the one to be

101

judged here, my brother. If anything, I should be the one who should be judged."

"Pino, now you're being a goof! You're being absolutely ridiculous!"

"Arturo, I murdered people for profit! If anything, I am the one who will be reaped by the Devil himself first and foremost! Out of my old greed and status, I murdered people to fill my own pockets. I was a lost soul, Arturo! I then saw my mistakes. I was living an empty life! Sometimes I miss that empty life!"

"Pino, please!"

"I do! I was lost, but now I was found, Arturo! You have brought me to the light, my dear brother. God bless you and all your goodness! We do not need an Inquisition, a commander, or an emperor! We only need to have goodness within our hearts! We only need to protect the children from the clutches of death! We are the soldiers that fight for life, Brother Arturo. We will fight for what is good until the very end as children of the light! And with that, I say, '*Benedictus pacis!*'"

Arturo smiled and silently praised, *"Benedictus pacis."*

Arturo took a bite of his meal and looked out into the sea. He looked hard and squinted. He saw something. He saw a small glowing red light. It disappeared and then reappeared. It loomed in the distance along the shoreline, approximately five hundred yards out. Through the thick fog, it continued to stalk the two Travelers.

"Pino, look over there," nudged Arturo. Pino turned over. He squinted and saw the red light. His eyes widened.

"Damn it," Pino exclaimed. "We have company! Kill the flames!"

"Who are they, Pino? Do you think they are one of ours?"

"It could be the prince, for all I care. We need to hide now!" Arturo and Pino dumped their water into the beautiful roaring fire and stomped on it until it was completely dead. They closed their travel bags and hid behind a grotto of trees. They saw the glowing red light become bigger and brighter as it reached closer to the island's beaches. What was formerly a brilliant red light soon transformed into a metal boat that held red glowing light on the top of its bow. The ship looked rusted but reliable. It was unlike any ship design that Arturo had ever seen. It was long, narrow, and sleek. It was painted a dark blue but featured its name on the side. The ship read *TECUMSEH* in scrawled red writing. Four silhouettes touched the island's beach and climbed the rocky shore. They held major assault artillery in their hands. They looked angry.

"Damn it, those are Indig pirates," whispered Pino. "They must have followed us after the firefight. We're dead."

"Shhh, they won't find us, brother," said Arturo. "We need to be quiet."

Arturo and Pino watched the pirates march down the grass, armed to the teeth and ready to kill. In the foggy darkness, Arturo could see them closely. They all had handsome features. They had elegant noses, beautiful copper skin, but piercing dark eyes that searched for their prey. Their eyes and face were painted various colors, each representing their own personality and character.

"The fire was around here," said a tall Indigenous man in his native tongue.

"They must be hiding. Search over by the brush, Beaver with No Tail. Gentle Leaf and Spider, go look over at the trees over there." The leader pointed towards Arturo and Pino's direction. Pino silently loaded his pistol and waited. Arturo did the same. They turned for a moment and saw that the pirate had disappeared within the fog. Pino and Arturo silently scanned the area. The crickets then stopped chirping.

Then Arturo and Pino turned. Within the blink of an eye, a pirate hit Arturo on the head with the hilt of his rifle, as did the other with Pino. They hooted and hollered in excitement. The pirates brought out ropes, tied their hands, and gagged their mouths with a cloth.

"Looks like we're getting a hot meal in Salem, boys." said the female leader excitedly. Her crew whooped in excitement and raised their rifles in glory. Their hair blew in the wind as they pointed their weapons at the two Travelers. They

laughed. Pino muffled in protest and tried to wriggle out of his constraints. The captors laughed.

"You boys probably don't understand what we're saying, so we'll speak in your Latin tongue," said the female leader smartly to Arturo and Pino. "It's not every day that we get to catch not only Latins but also Travelers. I know a Traveler when I see one. You sure are something else. Your emperor barely recognizes you, yet you try to 'help' other people. Good news: we don't need your help. But you're gonna help us."

The Travelers muffled in protest.

"*Beaver, Spider, shut them up, please*," asked the leader calmly to her partners. Her partners then grabbed the two by the hair roughly, brandished a knife, and pressed it firmly on the base of their scalp inches from making an incision.

"Tonight, we are going to sell you. We're going to sell you with a good price on your head, given how healthy you both look. Good bones, fresh blood, well-fed. I can smell the gold from here." Her friends laughed. She continued, "I am feeling generous tonight, so I know the perfect client to take you two off

106

my hands. Cooperate with us, and we will loosen your ropes a little bit on the way. Understood?"

Arturo and Pino muffled in protest again. The leader smiled and gave a gesture ending the conversation. Her crew whooped and cried and roughly dragged the two onto their ship. The band tied them to the middle of the boat and put them in chains. Pino kept fighting, but Arturo looked at him, urging him to stop fighting. The pirates went through their bags and admired all the new booty they had just acquired. They sang songs of their tongue and celebrated the momentous occasion of the Travelers' capture. They saw the fog break and shimmer away as if walking through a thick veil, as their ship sailed through the dark Atlantic Sea. In the distance, they saw glimmering lights and various ships docked across the massive shoreline. They saw the glorious, gargantuan mainland. Arturo and Pino finally reached the shores of America. They were now in the belly of the beast. The leader smirked and chuckled at the bewilderment of the Travelers.

"Gentlemen, welcome to Salem!"

9

The wind hollered as the *TECUMSEH* soared through the black waters of the Atlantic. Arturo and Pino shook in their shoes as the small ship landed on the Salem Harbor. Various ships of all shapes, sizes, and flags went to and from the sea, crossing different rivers and oceans to exchange goods from Northern or Southern America. However, the docks were lively and colorful. Arturo could hear strange music and singing as the Salemites carried their exotic goods and spices to and from the foreign ships. Bright torches and lights illuminated the black waters. The docks were centuries old but miraculously stood in place. Arturo observed the Salemite witches and was ultimately perplexed. He was surrounded by witches.

The Salemites were exotic-looking by design, given that they were all inherently nude or scantily clothed. Arturo, Pino, and the pirates stood out like sore thumbs, fully clothed. Arturo tried his best to avert his eyes to the ground in reverence but couldn't help but be mesmerized by the overt sexualization of the Americans. The lack of modesty in such a public place, a shipping pier of all places. Clothing seemed optional in Salem. Arturo noticed that the workers were primarily women but enjoyed their work. They sang strange songs about the earth and stars. They sang hymns thanking what they called Horned Father and cackled in the tall moonlight. They smiled and worked as if they were playing a child's game. Spider then pushed Arturo to keep moving. They continued walking.

Arturo witnessed the complexity of the city of Salem. They walked on cobblestone streets lit by streamers of light and lamp posts illuminated by candlelight. All the buildings were a mix of wood, stone, and steel. They were around seven to ten stories high, but it looked as if multiple houses were stacked on top of one another. Arturo heard the clopping of horses and mules, as well as the honking of automobiles, but those were a rare sight. The automobiles were bulbous and carriage-like. They looked similar to early models of automobiles that Arturo's great-great-grandfather had invented. They were black, with wooden and rubber wheels and two levers that would determine the vehicle's direction and another to control the speed. It was archaic yet efficient. He witnessed the chaos of the devilish urban landscape as he was escorted by the pirates.

Arturo saw people overtly kissing and promiscuously touching one another in the open streets. He witnessed a female Salemite, raven-haired, copper skin with blue eyes, holding hands with another witch who had golden hair, freckled shoulders who kissed her partner's neck seductively. Her partner then stopped dead in her pace, looked at her partner, and publicly kissed her. Such actions would result in instant punishment if they were back in Inquisitional Europe. They would wish they were killed under the hands of the Inquisition. Homosexuality and promiscuity would result in instantaneous death in Europe. However, this was the least of Arturo's worries.

Arturo witnessed more of what he saw as Sodom and Gomorrah as he continued pacing across the fiendish city. The crew then passed a marketplace where various old Salemites bartered and sold wild goods and services. A wave of smells of strange perfumes, incense, and manure intoxicated Arturo and the crew. Dogs and cats scurried under the crowded citizens' feet. A group of children ran across the streets giggling and pointing at the clothed Arturo and Pino. They wore colorful smocks and pointed hats and spoke a strange language amongst each other. Pino recalled some of the languages. It sounded a bit Germanic, but it wasn't. It sounded a bit like Latin, but far from it. He recalled a group once known as the English speaking a similar language. He thought it was a dead language. The young witches spoke in strange tongues as they taunted the captured duo.

One of the girls had long red hair. She was fair in complexion but almost as white as parchment paper. She had misty green eyes and a toothy grin, missing a front tooth. The red-haired child witch wore a bright green tunic with a belt that held a protective rune. She was probably eight years old. Closed tightly to her chest was a faceless stuffed poppet that wore a tunic identical to hers. She hugged it close and kissed it in the reassurance of all the chaos as if she were a worried mother closely protecting her kin from any potential danger. She was then pushed by a passing gentleman lumbering a herd of camels.

She fell into the dirty mud-caked streets and dropped her poppet. She cried, and the poppet was kicked in Arturo's direction and landed directly at his feet. He then leaned over and picked up the bonnet. His captors pushed him to move forward, but he ignored them. He then bent down on one knee to the witch and presented her poppet. She smiled and hugged her baby doll in thanks. She then looked at his mustache, gave it a quick pet, and giggled.

"I know you," she said dreamily. "I have seen you before." She then ran away and disappeared into the crowd, leaving Arturo confused but more at ease. The young witch reminded him of his children. Thoughts of his children began to swim in his mind until they were interrupted by Spider, who urged him to move forward by cocking his rifle.

"You'll get to know the locals more later. Lucky for you, you came at the best time of the year! Today's the Summer Solstice and they will need a few sacrifices to appease their horned god. Keep moving."

Arturo looked at the various market stands. They sold and presented unusual goods and services. Arturo saw exotic animals, birds, and reptiles, big and small, in cages or passing through the streets. Bears and lions roared in annoyance, demanding their release. A man in a turban and loosely fitted silks paraded himself on an ornately dressed elephant. The elephant trumpeted as various Salemites admired in awe or in dull passing. A woman held a snake around her neck and appeared to be having an amusing conversation with her scaly friend. A young chubby boy was seen holding a toad asking the toad to remind him what his mother wanted him to buy in the market.

In the distance, a male witch wearing only a scarf and pointed hat gave a tattoo to a young mohawked man with a braided beard on his chest. The symbol was a green-inked rune of protection. Blood poured over the young man's chest, but he gave an expression of strength and resilience. He smiled a seductive grin at Pino and winked. Pino turned away quickly and continued walking. Arturo and Pino saw a young Arabic woman with long hair reaching her waist and wearing multiple rings, necklaces, and bracelets, selling silk scarves and candles to a teenage boy. She presented a mirror to the young customer and posed in front of it.

"My darling, this will match your eyes! Look at the blueness of this material! It only allows your beauty to shine even brighter! Only the finest silk from Virginia! It will bring you many, many lovers! Oh, how you must purchase it!"

The young boy admired himself. He had curly dark hair, smooth skin, cherub-like lips, and long eyelashes. He was tall, lanky, but incredibly handsome. He posed in the mirror and had a rush of self-confidence consume him. He smiled, reached into his pocket, and gave the Arabic witch three silver coins. He then wore it and walked away with a confident smile.

Arturo and Pino turned white. The duo saw a hobbled crone chopping meat in a butcher shop. She was sweaty, hands caked with blood, and had hairs sprouting from her chin. Her hair was grizzled gray and drenched in sweat. Flies hung around her face, but she seemed unbothered. However, it wasn't just any butcher shop. Hanging from its stand were the corpses of infants. Human infants. Headless infant corpses hung upside down like freshly slaughtered poultry. Presented on the table were the skulls of various babies of all shapes and sizes. The teeth of the babies were seen offered as multiple necklaces and bracelets. Vials of blood ointments were a hot commodity. A young witch bartered with the crone. The crone grunted at the young witch's propositions. When presented with the right price, the crone smiled a toothless smile, nodded, and opened her hands with a small bag full of gold coins. Cries were heard in the back of the butcher stand. The pirate leader laughed.

"You know all those stories about missing children?" she explained. "Consider that a black market deal. Babies from the Inquisition are stolen and sold here in Salem and throughout the country. Baby's blood is precious to these witches. Need to protect yourself from nightmares? Get a baby teeth necklace. Trying to protect yourself from an apparition? Eat the flesh of a baby. Want to fly with the Devil and his children? Bathe yourself in baby blood. All missing children end up here in Salem. We're just about here."

10

Excitement filled the great city of Salem. Music was in the air. The night of rituals was upon them. The crew stopped and saw what was Salem's city center. People crowded the streets with their buggies and carts. They all would look upon and pay reverence to what appeared to be a black marble obelisk. The obelisk was surrounded by four different iron poles that faced the north, the south, the east, and the west. The poles were surrounded by hay, wood, and other various materials. The obelisk had images that featured the history of Salem engraved onto the stone from images of ships landing on the uninhabited land of Salem. The image then transitioned to a group of Salemite Puritans kneeling before a cross in tears and fear, shielding themselves before the heavenly light. Then it transitioned to a woman of African descent, an old man that resembled a pilgrim, and three young girls, all of whom were kneeling towards a perfect-looking man with the head of a ram.

Soon images of violence, blood, and infanticide were shown on the gargantuan obelisk. The monument presented a story of bloodshed and progress. It explained how Salem and the rest of the North American continent spat at the faces of their Christian oppressors and built their own utopia. They built a utopia under mercy of the Devil himself.

Behind the obelisk was a significant building that resembled a grand temple. Instead of images of the Greek gods, various devilish creatures and witches throughout American history that Arturo and Pino knew nothing of were engraved on the monument. Three hundred years of history were utterly foreign to the men of God. Arturo was utterly taken aback and overwhelmed with such complexity of the architecture. The pirates entered the building, and various other strange, untrustworthy individuals waited in a long line with other captured individuals. They waited for a few moments until they were called next in line and presented to a group of three middle-aged women in a single room. They sat on elevated podiums, looking down upon their subjects.

"Kneel before the High Priestesses of Salem!"

announced a distant voice from a nearby balcony speaking the strange Salemite language. Beneath them, armed female guards stood in protection of their witchy politicians. Arturo and Pino were forced to kneel before three stern-looking women. One was plump, tired-looking, and resembled a briar. The other resembled a scarecrow covered with various scars. The third was pleasant and young-looking. She had long dark hair, tanned skin, and was petite. She looked like a young bird about to leap off her first branch. She had a look of fairness and reasonability. She sat in the center of the room between the other two witch priestesses. Beside her was a little girl with bright red hair who looked awfully familiar, but Arturo could not make out her face because they were so far away.

"Pirate crew of the TECUMSEH*, what sacrifices do you present to the court for this coming Summer Solstice,"* asked the young high priestess in her strange language.

The leader and her crew bowed in reverence. *"My crew and I are humbled to be in your presence, High Priestess Sara*

Adamson," said the leader of the *TECHUMSEH*. "*Salem has treated my people with great respect and with open arms. In thanks, we present to you these two men. Catholics they are, my lady.*"

"*We are given many Catholics as sacrifices, young lady,*" said High Priestess Adamson sternly. "*We are given many prisoners of war that enter this room. We have enough for thirteen solstices. What makes these men worthy of your price? The court knows you can be quite expensive, Captain Mayflower. They might as well be sent to work camps in the Carolinas with the others.*"

"*My High Priestesses, I can assure you that these men are not your ordinary Catholics. They are Travelers! Missionaries that travel far and wide to spread the word of the Catholic god. They are outcasts of their society. Therefore, they are special! They also escaped a firefight from my brothers and sisters who defeated the legendary* Archangel*!*"

The courtroom attendants gasped. The high priestesses and the other witnesses whispered to themselves in shock.

119

"Silence," exclaimed Adamson angrily. *"I will not have such lies in my court! You are to be dismissed with no pay. Take them out of my sight,"* exclaimed High Priestess Adamson boldly. *"They are wasting my time."*

Arturo could pick up some of the words they gathered from their strange language. He remembered learning this dead language back in university, but he was never fluent. He rattled his chains and stood before the court. "We did escape them, your honor!" Arturo shouted. He was then dragged by Spider, but Arturo shoved him away. Arturo approached the bench valiantly. The guards stood ready to attack, but High Priestess Adamson raised her hand to stop their advance.

"Do go on, sir. What is your Catholic name?" she asked. Adamson's Latin shocked Arturo for a moment. Arturo was impressed with her fairness. He gave the priestess a look of thankfulness and urgency.

"Forgive me, madam, I am not familiar with your language, but I will do my best to communicate to the court. My name is Dr. Arturo…Butera, your honor. I am a simple Traveler.

This is my fellow Traveler and holy brother, Giuseppe. And yes, we both survived and escaped the *Archangel*."

"Who attacked your ship, Doctor?"

"My ship was attacked by a fleet of Indigenous submarines, my lady. My brother and I were held captive by the Inquisitional authorities known as the HOWs."

"We know of the HOWs. By the name of the Horned Father, we curse their name. But do continue, Dr. Butera."

"We were taken prisoner by the Inquisitional authorities while we were on our mission in South Africa."

"Were you aware of the reasons why the HOWs interrupted your mission? Surely, the most secretive branch of the Inquisition would not choose any person without a purpose."

Arturo's stomach began to tighten. He hated lying. He always hated lying. He looked at Pino for reassurance, and the same look of panic formed before his eyes as well. Arturo began to turn red, and silence hung in the air like a noose as the council waited for Arturo's answer. He had to give an answer. They would surely kill him if he refused. Arturo opened his mouth to answer, but a small whisper came from the balcony where the High Priestess Adamson sat. Her daughter was speaking to her mother. Adamson chuckled.

"*Mamma, it is not funny! I know him*!" said the red-haired girl in her Salemite tongue.

"Rosie don't be ridiculous, darling," responded Adamson in Latin. "You don't know him, my love."

"Yes, I do!" exclaimed Rosie. "I met him in the market today when I was with my friends! I dropped my baby, and he gave it to me."

"That is very nice of him, darling, but that doesn't mean that you know him. You just crossed paths with him."

"No, Mamma! I saw him in my dreams!"

The room became quiet for a moment. Silence hung in the air for a few moments. "Honey, that is very, very different," said Adamson. "You know how important your dreams are! Let the court note that my daughter, Rosie Adamson, will be making a statement on my behalf. Go ahead, darling, tell the court your dream."

Rosie then took a step down and walked toward Arturo and Pino nervously. She then looked at Arturo's kind eyes and smiled, gaining encouragement and confidence. Rosie continued,

"For the past few nights, I have been dreaming about him. I had a dream that I was standing in a meadow by the sea, and he was looking out at the sea. A white flower grew next to me when I saw him. He turned around and smiled at me. And then I woke up."

"What does this have to prove?" asked Spider, annoyed.

"I think he is important! I don't think we should kill him."

"*You are absolutely right,*" said Adamson boldly transitioning to her native language. "*Because my daughter is the seventh child of the seventh child, we must take her omen seriously. We must protect and house this man because he may restore greatness and prosperity for not only Salem but the entirety of America! We are on the brink of war! We are blessed*

by the Horned Father to have this Catholic outcast further

restore our greatness and help us destroy the hazardous

Catholic nation once and for all! He does not know our ways of

life. I volunteer to educate Dr. Butera and take him personally to

our home. My wife Cathleen, Rosie, and I will teach him the

ways. He will speak our language! He will enroll in our schools,

walk amongst us, live amongst us. This man will bring our

nation to fruition. He will become a proud citizen of America."

Arturo had no way to process this plan. It was absolutely

ridiculous, mad even! Never in his wildest dreams would he

have imagined himself not only in America once again but to

live amongst the squander of the so-called hags. Images of his

family and Roberto swam in his head again. He felt that he was

going straight to the fiery inferno for just merely standing in this

room. Arturo wanted to escape more than anything. He tried to

take Pino back home to Cassino with him. Arturo wanted to kiss

his Antoinetta, Bruna, Rocco, Mario, and Anita again.

"Are you out of your damn minds?" Pino spat as he charged for the high priestesses. "Arturo is not going to live with you filthy hags! He will not submit to your horrendous ways of this godforsaken rock! By God, I thought the Inquisition was good at this brainwashing bullshit, but you make it look like an art! We are innocent! We want nothing to do with this war! We want nothing to do, you filthy b–"

Pino then stopped his banter and his face turned bright red. He gasped for air. He then fell over and kicked his legs and flailed his arms. His eyes looked as if they were ready to pop from his head.

"Mr. Giuseppe, I will assure you that your holy brother will be in good hands," said Adamson boldly. "Under my roof, he will receive the best care possible as if he were your Pope himself. Because you are so unwilling to our ways, the court will sentence you to death by hanging."

"Let him go," Arturo yelled, kneeling beside him. "He is innocent! For my sake, please spare him! I promise I will live and follow your ways! But for the love of all things good, spare my friend."

High Priestess Adamson thought long and hard for a moment. Pino began turning an ugly shade of blue. She waved her hand, and Pino finally took a gasp of air. He coughed and hacked. Pino's eyes rolled and passed out cold. Arturo checked his pulse. He was still alive. High Priestess Adamson then stood to give the charges:

"Mr. Giuseppe Alessandro, under the care of the Council of Salem, under the eye of the Council of the Ram, and under the grasp of Satan, you are hereby sentenced to fifteen years in a work camp in the Carolinas, located in the Province of the Toad. As for Dr. Arturo Butera, under the care of the Council of Salem, under the eye of the Council of the Ram, and under the grasp of Satan, you are hereby spared to be a sacrifice from the Summer Solstice, under the conditions of precognition. You will be immediately relocated to the Adamson household for temporary living for the purposes of reeducation. Council adjourned. Welcome to Salem, Dr. Butera."

11

The evening boomed with life and excitement as the citizens of Salem prepared for the night's festivities. Salemites wore their best silks and scarves. They put on their best pointed hats and painted their faces in various symbols and runes to bless them and their evening. Music hung in the air with witches playing bagpipes, pipes, horns, drums, and flutes. They danced exotic dances with no rhyme or rhythm. Their eyes rolled as they felt the music channel their soul throughout their body. People paraded down the main streets of Salem. Smells of food and sweat lifted the air. Offerings of slaughtered pigs and doves splattered the streets with blood. Tonight was the night of the Devil.

Arturo's shackles were removed. He was then gently escorted by an old witch to another room. She was a portly woman, with a round face, rosy cheeks, and a button for a nose. She had curly gray-white hair and a beautiful smile, despite having little to no teeth. She wore a long dark purple skirt but no upper garments. Her bare breasts sagged as she moved quickly to serve Arturo. She was called Orla.

The room was quaint but elegant. It resembled a hotel room similar to the ones Arturo had seen in Rome. It had red carpets, ornate but simple furniture, and a beautiful mural that depicted a mountainous desert landscape. It was yellow, dusty, but so vast. The mural depicted a purple sky that gave the yellow rocky terrain a slightly orange hue.

"That be the Rockies, Master Butera," said Orla, chuckling at Arturo's curiosity. "Observant, are you?"

"Yes, madam, I am fascinated by this landscape," said Arturo quietly. "By God, is it fantastic! Is it real, or is it purely fictional?"

"Oh, it's real all right, Master Butera. That be out west in the Province of the Snake. Beautiful land! So vast and untouched. Blessed by the Devil, I would say. Picture thousands of miles of endless mountains and valleys! Picture millions of trees that fill the air!"

"God, this continent is massive."

"Indeed it is, Master Butera. The Christians wanted it, but we claimed it. There is so much to this country than you could possibly imagine. The world is a lot bigger than you think. You will learn our geography, history, and our ways."

"Apparently, I will. And I will agree with you, madam. This is unlike anything I had ever imagined. I must say that your Latin is phenomenal."

"A dead language it is here, Master Butera. The Inquisition reaped all languages and knowledge from the Western World, all except here. Here, we speak our forefathers' English tongue. My great-gran was a Catholic and a witch in secret back in Ireland. The Inquisition tried to kill her, but she thankfully escaped and moved here to Salem. My family has lived a bountiful life here in Salem. That is why I still keep a Latin tongue."

"I thought you were a slave to High Priestess Adamson?"

"I am not, Master Butera. I simply serve the Adamson family, as my family has for generations since our immigration to America. They are a good family, sire. They will treat you well. And do call her Goody Adamson. She and Lady Cathleen will greatly appreciate it."

"Will do, madam."

"Wonderful," she exclaimed, completely ignoring Arturo's overwhelming fear and curiosity. "We must prepare you for the festivities for the evening! Please remove your shift that way, you will look presentable to the Horned Father."

"Remove my what?"

Orla grabbed Arturo by the hand and led him to another unknown location. He was bathed and pampered in colorful green and gold pants, shirtless, but covered in a red fleece cape draped over him. A gold laurel hung on his head. He thought he looked absolutely ridiculous. He felt like a real simp. He thought how Pino would probably make fun of him, saying how he resembled Emperor Nero because of how stupid he looked. Arturo smelled strange, like strange oils and incense. It burned his nose as he tried to rub off the strange perfume from his skin in sly disgust. However, the pants and cape were quite comfortable.

Orla and Arturo paced across a long and narrow hallway. Hanging from the walls were portraits of past High Priestesses. Towards the very end of the hallway turned one bigger and grander than the rest. It featured an indigenous woman with long braids, a handsome nose, and simple brown garbs while wearing a red turban-like head-wrap. Under it, a golden tag was placed:

Tituba

1674 - 1774

Orla opened a balcony door, and there was a patio filled with ornately dressed politicians. Never would Arturo imagine that these people would not only worship the Devil but also possess the ability to politic. Throughout his life, he had known these witches to be unreasonable heathen savages that would kill him without any mercy. They would kill him for simply loving Christ and His teachings. He saw various important figures as they held beautiful chalices and whispered amongst themselves as he was led toward the edge of the balcony. The majority of the politicians were female, elderly, but ceremoniously dressed, representing their background, culture, and province. Three women of African descent wearing gorgeous white dresses, white turbans, and leopard skin shawls whispered to one another and scoffed Arturo.

"They are voodoo priestesses of the Province of the Toad," whispered Orla. "They are known for their animal and human sacrifices. They often provide us with live animal and human sacrifice trade throughout the country. They are major traders for the continent. They practice Voodoo, the oldest presentation of the Horned Father. They are the second wealthiest of the nation."

They fanned themselves with peacock feathers as the summer breeze brushed them. Arturo saw three muscular men wearing various bear furs and stood practically naked. Their skins were ceremoniously caked in blood and earth. They had a look of wildness in their eyes as they viciously glared into Arturo's soul.

"Those are warriors from the Province of the Raven," explained Orla. "They are descended from Celts, Scandinavians, and Mongols. They hunt bison with the Indigenous colonies. They are known for their strength and resilience. They do not contribute much to Salem, but they are still recognized. They are quite independent. Some say they wish to make their land their own country, but I find it highly unlikely it will happen. I would suggest staying away from them. They are known to bite the throats of those who insult them."

Three women of Asian descent dressed in colorful reptilian scales and furs, hoods over their heads with elegant makeup, giggled as Arturo fidgeted his cape and loosely fit pants. Having no undergarments made him incredibly uncomfortable and exposed.

"Those are sorceresses from the Province the Snake. They come from the Eastern side of the world. They are known for their mysterious arts and medicine. They are incredibly beneficial to Salem."

Arturo and Orla then saw High Priestess Adamson and her fellow priestesses. They were chatting with someone who appeared to be an Indigenous politician. He wore a colorful beige outfit lovingly decorated with colorful beads. On top of his mighty head wore a grand eagle feathered headdress. He stood tall and proud. Instead, he did not speak but listened to Adamson as she quietly discussed politics with him.

"And you have obviously met Goody Adamson. She is one of the High Priestesses of the Province of the Ram and the Mayor of the grand city of Salem. Beside her would be Chief Sitting Bear of the Northern Indigenous American Confederation," said Orla excitedly. "He is the paramount chief of all Native tribes throughout Northern America reaching as far as the Arctic Circle. He is a very powerful man. His people helped us tremendously in the past during the harsh winters. They ensured our forefathers' survival. Shame the Christians had to spit at his people in the face. Never bite the hand that feeds you. His people later helped us take our land away from the Christians. They helped purge every firstborn Puritan who defied them and us. Thus, creating our eternal peace between them. Thus, starting this war. Come, Master Butera, we must join Goody Adamson."

Arturo then swallowed. His throat went dry, and he grew pale. His head began to spin. He was surrounded by warlords and heathens. They were his sworn enemies, yet he was welcomed like a comrade. Orla saw his uneasiness and handed Arturo a silver chalice and pushed him in the direction of Goody Adamson. Goody Adamson was dressed in elegant silks of black and gold. She wore a laurel similar to Arturo's. Her hair was draped over one side of her shoulders. She smiled and laughed as Chief Sitting Bear chuckled. Her eyes then met with Arturo, and she gave him a firm hug and a kiss on the cheek as if they were long-lost friends. It was as if she had forgotten of the turmoil that occurred in the previous hours of the evening.

"Dr. Butera! We are so glad you could make it! You have been the talk of the town this evening."

Arturo formed a small but disingenuous smile, masking his immense fear and anxiety. He felt as if he were the prophet Daniel in the lions' den. Arturo wanted to go on his knees and openly ask God to help him leave this dangerous place. He was surrounded by evil. The land was so foreign and strange. Their kindness and hospitality were strange yet familiar. He felt empty. They reminded him of the award ceremonies Arturo's father would take him to when the Archbishop of Rome would award his father for his technological innovation and devotion to the Inquisition. He recalled meeting various strange faces that would berate and taunt him, making him feel small and weak. He tried his best to gain his composure. He gave a fake grin and took a sip of his chalice.

"Well, I am incredibly honored to be here, high priestess," said Arturo in his best cheerful tone. "You are looking radiant this evening."

"Why, thank you, Dr. Butera! May I have the honor of introducing the paramount chief of the Northern Indigenous Confederation, Chief Sitting Bear."

"Pleasure to meet you, sir. An honor to meet you."

The chief nodded, smiled a small smile, but studied Arturo closely with his fierce dark eyes. His eyes seemed to have seen many battles. Arturo noticed a large scar on his left cheek and his left ear was completely missing. Arturo shook the chief's hands. They were rough like sandpaper.

"As it is to meet you, Dr. Butera. You are going to bring great things for us, I have heard. My people believe in prophecy as well. Despite us not sharing the same faiths as our witch allies, we support them diplomatically as a joint effort to prevent the Catholics from setting foot onto our lands again. They slaughtered our people and have tried to take away our ways of life, Doctor. We must do the same but with a greater force. You can be our voice as well. We must discuss future plans on how you can also help our people, doctor. Don't ever be a stranger."

"I must say, my lord," Arturo said respectfully. "Your Latin is incredible!"

"Thank you, Doctor! When I was a boy, my family was captured by the Inquisition and we were put in their re-education program. We were taught your language and forced to learn your ways. I escaped, leaving this pretty mark on my face."

Sitting Bear then brandished his horribly scarred face. Arturo winced at the grotesque scarification. The chief then gave a light chuckle and patted Arturo on the back. Goody Adamson gazed at the sky. She looked as if she were reading the stars and their position. She then raised her chalice and clinked it. The chatter amongst the politicians lowered.

"Ladies and gentlemen, the Summer Solstice is about to begin," announced Goody Adamson pleasantly. "Please grab your chalices and stand on the edge of the balcony."

Arturo stood beside Goody Adamson. She held his arm as if walking down the aisle of a wedding. Arturo waited for a speech to be given by one of the politicians. Instead, they gazed upon the city's center. Thousands of people stood below them, surrounding the inner circle. All were playing music and singing strange hymns, dancing provocatively on the streets. Arturo looked down and observed the obelisk. The monument stood in all its gargantuan terror upon the crowd. The front doors of the temple swung open. Immediately, the crowd grew silent. The crowd was so quiet that one could hear a pin drop.

Arturo saw three elderly witches exiting the front doors of the temple. Arturo had seen many elderly witches in passing, but none were as old as these women. The three sisters looked beyond ancient. Their skin was as wrinkled as ancient papyrus. Their hair was barely present. The sisters were barefoot and only wore skirts and ceremonious pointed hats. They ceremoniously hobbled across a red carpet that led them towards the city center's obelisk. Behind them was a person entirely covered in a white cloak who carried a large golden bowl with them. The cloaked figure presented the witches with the golden bowl. They danced around the obelisk while smearing a dark red ointment on their decaying flesh. The ointment appeared to be blood. They continued dancing around the obelisk in unison. Then a large flame enveloped the surrounding obelisk. The flame roared with life, and the images of the obelisk were illuminated. Silent chants began to grow. Chants that could not be recognized by any ear throughout the world, a chant created before time itself. It was a chant for Satan.

The three sisters continued their dancing and chanting. A powerful tribal drum began to play at a slow tempo. The witches moved in unison to the rhythm.

"They are the Sisters of Old," whispered Goody Adamson. "They are as old as time itself. They are the keepers of our ways. Some say they taught the druids of the Britains their ways. Others say they were the first to write their name in the Horned Father's book. Tonight they must perform a ritual for the Summer Solstice. They must do this to thank the Horned Father for all the gifts he has given us. Watch."

The powerful drum then began playing at a faster tempo. The witches then began following the rhythm and danced faster. They then dropped to their knees and began speaking in tongues. Their eyes rolled to the back of their head. The audience continued silently chanting the hymn in unison. They then collapsed in a state of animalistic motion. They growled and hissed. Multiple voices emerged from their lips. The sisters' bodies began convulsing uncontrollably. The Devil was within them.

A young woman then appeared. She stood completely naked, had auburn hair, and looked utterly nervous. She looked willing but insecure. She took a deep breath and walked towards the dancing sisters. She ceremoniously stepped in the beat of the drum's temple and laid on the ground in the middle of the convulsing weird sisters. The drum began beating louder, and the chants increased. They grew louder and louder. The sisters then turned to the young woman and, like wild animals, began tearing the poor girl's flesh. Using their pointed sharp teeth, they devoured her soft flesh. The poor girl's eyes rolled back, and her body began to jolt and contort as the sisters feasted upon her flesh. As the chants grew louder, Arturo saw something that he would never forget for the rest of his days. The three sisters began to levitate!

As the sisters rose higher and higher, the crowd went into a fit of crazed ecstasy. They cried and moaned as a wicked congregation. They bore witness to the levitating sisters. They began singing unified praises. They praised their Horned Father and his many names. They praised Papa Legba. They praised Loki. They praised Lucifer. All names dedicated to the Horned

Father. As the witches rose higher and higher, the crowd cried and bowed. The Devil was present with Arturo. He could feel his icy breath on his neck. Blood dripped to the ground as the witches continued to levitate.

The cloaked figure went underneath the wicked feast that suspended into the air. Blood dripped and stained the white cloak. He made sure to cover it with every last drop. The witches then soon began to descend to the mortal earth. The drums started slowing their tempo, as did the audience's chants, until there was complete silence. The young girl's body was completely mangled, half-eaten, and raw. Her eyes stood open as her corpse was brought gently to the ground by the sisters. One of them closed the girl's eyes. The cloaked figure then ceremoniously laid the white cloak over a stone tabernacle. He read the bloodied veil and raised his hands. He shouted from the top of his lungs:

"BEWARE, THE MAN OF THE FIELDS IS NEAR!

BEWARE THE MAN OF SILVER THAT IS HERE!

FOR HE SHALL BEAR THE BEAST'S MARK!

HE SHALL END THE LIGHT AND DARK!

FOR THE HEAD OF THE RAM MAY FALL!

GODS AND CITIES, DEAD WILL BE ALL!"

Arturo then stood numb again. He now knew that there was no
escape from this wretched place.

This was only the beginning.

12

The ritual seemed like a distant dream to Arturo. He looked out the window of his cottage. Red, orange, and yellow leaves delicately brushed against his window. The October breeze whirled and twirled as the winds bid Arturo good morning, urging him to start his daily routine. Like a child, he knelt on his bed and looked out the window longingly. He observed the outside world that was and will possibly forever be his prison. The world of America seemed large and vast. He was a stranger in a strange room, trapped in a strange world.

He crawled to the floorboard of the corner of his bedroom, underneath his rug. With a pencil that he held behind his ear, he lifted the wooden plank with ease, ever so quietly so as not to alert or awaken anyone within the house. He had to be careful. Inside were his prized possessions. One was a photograph of his family. He looked at it for a moment. Lovingly caressing it, his heart began to flutter. Using his vivid and brilliant imagination, Arturo pictured himself with his family. He no longer wore his silly cloaks and boots. He no longer smelled of strange incense. He no longer witnessed works of the Devil. He imagined himself on his wedding day where hundreds of people bore witness to him and his lovely bride, Antoinetta, joining together in infinite love. Her eyes shined as did her smile. Her white veil over her lovely face was immaculate. His heart began to flutter as the daydream began to shift to his children. He pictured their holidays in the Italian countryside. He pictured running along the beaches, carrying his youngest daughter, Anita, in one arm and his youngest boy, Mario, on the other, as he raced his other two older children, Bruna and Rocco. They laughed and screamed with delight. He saw Antonietta under an umbrella sitting on a beach blanket laughing hysterically. She glowed with happiness and love. Arturo's heart began to soar further until he heard footsteps approach his door. He quickly but carefully set the photograph down. Next to the picture was his other prized possession: the pocket watch.

Arturo then grabbed the nearest book and pretended to be doing his studies. Orla opened the door. With her usual smiling face, she poked her head through the door.

"Good morrow, sire," she cooed, beaming with joy. "Today is a gorgeous day! It is Devil's Sabbath! Aren't you just thrilled?! You have grown so much since you first landed here in Salem. The Horned Father has been most pleased with you and your studies, I am sure of it! You do recall what we do on Devil's Sabbath, yes?"

"Yes, I do, Orla," said Arturo in his best cheerful morning tone. "It is the night where we celebrate the Horned Father. According to the books, they say that it is the night where he first tempted Adam and Eve and introduced them to the truth of humanity. He helped them bear witness to their true potential. He showed them that power and freedom are the answer to all humanity."

"My word! You have become quite the scholar! Oh, bless you!" beamed Orla as she gave Arturo a nice, wet kiss on the forehead. "Breakfast is ready, and Goody Adamson and Lady

Cathleen would love for you to join them. Little Rosie has requested that you take her to school today."

Arturo smiled a genuine smile. He had grown quite fond of Goody Adamson's little daughter, Rosie. Not only had she saved his life, but she also had helped him become more acclimated to Salem and their ways. She reminded Arturo of his little daughters. She was very kind, loving, and nothing like her mothers. Goody Adamson enrolled Arturo in the same school Rosie attended, and where her wife, Cathleen, was the headmaster of the school. The school was a large red wooden building located within the city, a long ride by carriage. The Adamson residence resided in the wealthier district of the city, which resembled a more suburban area with more trees and vegetation and less congestion of the scrappy urban landscape. Despite the size of Salem, there were only a few hundred children that resided in the city. Children were a rare sight in Salem. If only Salemites would stop eating them.

Arturo dressed in his boots and autumn cloak. He went down the grand staircase and met with his hosts in the dining room. Goody Adamson sat at the head of the table, reading various important documents as she bit into a slice of toast. Lady Cathleen sat on the opposite side, eating her eggs and ham. Rosie sat in between them, trying to encourage her poppet to eat her meal, despite possessing no mouth. Arturo sat opposite Rosie and smiled.

"Good morrow Goody Adamson, Lady Cathleen, and Lady Rosie. Happy Devil's Sabbath," Arturo announced politely as he sat down. He gave himself a moment to say a silent prayer in his head, thanking the Lord for his meal, and then proceeded to eat. Praying silently was his only way of feeling free. This defiance gave him a sliver of hope.

"Happy Devil's Sabbath, Doctor. Cathleen has told me that you have been passing your marks with flying colors! You are ensuring the future of this nation, Dr. Butera. I can assure you, we will bring glory to this nation!"

"Oh darling, no politics at the table," said Lady Cathleen smiling. "There is always room for politics tonight."

"There is always room for politics! We have the future of Salem and our nation sitting at our table!"

"Darling, please. Also, we need to prepare our home for the evening."

"Oh? We are hosting it here, at the house?" asked Arturo inquisitively. "Are we not doing the festivities in front of the city like the Summer Solstice?"

"Goodness no! Years ago, our forefathers would partake in the Devil's Sabbath as a whole city. However, that proved to be an absolute mess and disaster. Instead, we celebrate Devil's Sabbath with neighbors privately. Think of it as your Christmas holiday. It is meant to be celebrated with people you know and appreciate. Does that make sense?"

"Yes, Lady Cathleen. Thank you. Are you excited, little Rosie?"

"Oh, dear me! Rosie will not be joining us tonight. Instead, Rosie and all the other children will celebrate it differently from the adults. Devil's Sabbath is meant to come at a certain age later in life. Rosie is not ready for that. It is meant for those who have already signed their name to the Devil. That is usually around the age of 17. When she is of age, she will remove her shift for the first time, write her name in the Devil's book, and become, not only an official follower of the Horned Father, but also a woman. You remember your studies, don't you, Arturo."

"Yes, Lady Cathleen, I do."

"Good! Also, Rosie has requested that you would take her to school today. Would that be alright with you?"

"Of course! Whatever the little lady wishes, I would gladly provide."

"Also do be careful! There was a story on the news saying that there have been some zealots on the streets. Please be sure to stay away from them. There was a riot that broke out in the main square a few days ago. They claim that the end of the world is near, and we need to repent. They can be dangerous. Thankfully, Goody Adamson took care of the problem."

"Straight to the Carolinas they went," exclaimed Goody Adamson, sipping her tea. "I will not be having religious heathens on my street. I believe we can prevent this apocalypse, Doctor. I believe that this is our push for greatness. We need to destroy the Catholic nation to ensure our nation's survival."

"You are right, Goody Adamson," said Arturo, eating a slice of ham.

"Wonderful! You are dismissed."

***

"Let's practice your English, Doc," said Rosie holding Arturo's hand, swinging it playfully as they walked towards the school building.

"What would you like me to say, little flower?" asked Arturo sweetly.

"Hmmm," she thought as she looked at her surroundings of the buzzing city, thinking of an example for Arturo to answer. Her eyes then lit up, and she giggled. "Say 'you want to ride that pony, please.'"

"I would ride pony, please."

"Haha! You were so close," giggled Rosie.

Arturo laughed and lovingly pinched Rosie's tiny cheek. Arturo's Salemite English was still very poor, but he was improving. Their language was very guttural, unromantic, and violent. He missed speaking his Latin tongue. He missed his family. He missed Johannesburg and its people. He especially missed Pino. Every night he prayed for Pino. He often imagined him being tortured by his witch captors as he worked in the labor camps. He was forbidden to talk about Pino or his family. He didn't know if anyone he loved was dead or alive. That was one of the many conditions he was given when living in Salem and under the Adamson household.

He was always under a watchful eye whenever they left the household. Walking beside them was Calciph, Goody Adamson's cat familiar. Familiars were a common sight within Salem. Familiars were the companions of witches. They came from all shapes and sizes, ranging from field mice, ravens, cats, snakes, toads, or even mules.

"Tell me about the goat, Doc." quizzed Rosie giggling.

"Well, the most sacred animal within Salem is the black goat. The black goat is the physical embodiment of the Horned Father. He is known for his enormous, long black hair and incredible longhorns. There have been stories that he would change shape on the Devil's Sabbath. He would torture poor souls and have them submit to him to achieve eternal power, glory, and freedom. He lives in a large house behind the temple and is heavily guarded by a vast wall. He is said to be well-fed and drink the finest mead. He is sacred to the people of Salem."

"Good job, Doc! You're so smart!"

"I try my best, little flower. I try my best."

Arturo finally reached the school. Calciph climbed a nearby fence and monitored the pair closely. They walked into the building and down the school's short hallway. Rosie then tugged on Arturo's cloak and motioned for him to come closer. He then knelt down and lent an open ear.

"I am so happy you are here," she whispered sweetly and then gave him a hug. "You are my big brother."

Arturo returned the hug. He caressed her soft red hair. A small tear trickled down his face. Her sweetness reminded him of his children. She then looked behind Arturo's ear, touched the back of his ear, and tickled it.

"What are you doing, little flower?" asked Arturo, laughing at Rosie, as he quickly wiped away his tears.

"You have a funny mark behind your ear."

"Yes, of course, I have had it since birth. Why does it look bad?"

"No. It looks fine. I'm just thinking."

"What are you thinking about, Rosie?"

"Birthmarks mean important things. You are important. That mark means something big is going to happen to you."

She ran away to her classroom as the bell rang above Arturo.

13

The sun blazed upon the fields of the Carolinas. Cicadas whistled and sang in the nearby trees. Mosquitos buzzed around irritatingly, looking for fresh blood to drink. Corn stalks grew tall and proud, waiting to be picked by their slave harvesters. The grunts of slaves were heard throughout the cornfields. Songs of hope for a better life filled the hot Carolina air, as an incredibly skinny Pino scavenged the lavishly colored ears of corn.

Time had been lost for Pino. It seemed as if it were only yesterday that he had last seen Arturo in the devilish temple in Salem. He thought of his old friend, not knowing whether he was alive or dead. He tried to brush away all the possible thoughts and scenarios of his poor friend and how they would torture him. He imagined Arturo's captors tying him up to a dark, cold dungeon and giving him nothing but scraps. Pino imagined them torturing him but searing his flesh with an iron, drawing his blood for various potions and brews, or haunting him with their apparitions. He prayed that his dear brother was alive. Pino himself didn't know if he was alive or dead. For all he knew, he was in Hell.

Immediately when Pino was taken from the court, he and other prisoners of war were loaded onto a ship and sent to one of the most horrendous work camps in the Carolinas. The camp was called Camp Hale. The camp was approximately 842 acres of land, with fields upon fields of crops. Within the endless rows of fields were 80,000 prisoners picking, planting and hauling crops dedicated to the Horned Father's children. The prisoners were all naked while they worked, only wearing a cap and cloth to cover their shoulders and head from the sun. However, this innovation was discovered only a few seasons ago. Newcomers had their photo taken and were welcomed with a cruel white-hot iron that gave them their respective prison number. They were then deloused and taken to their cottage. The following morning, they would work until the sun set, eat, and start the day over again when the sun rose. They had no name. They had no life. They had no God.

The camp was run by a cruel woman by the name of Elizabeth Williams. She was the warden of this godforsaken camp who claimed that she descended from the great Abigail Williams, one of the founding forefathers of their supposedly great nation. However, her slave handlers silently found this unlikely. She had long dark hair that was put in a tight bun. She wore a long red sash that presented her title as warden and confidently rode naked on her black stallion, as she gazed upon what she thought was a beautiful sight. She lived to torture her Christian animals. They were her pets and instruments of torture. They were all hers.

Alongside her and scattered amongst the endless fields of the camp were the slave handlers. They, too, rode naked and on top of their horses. At their side were their loyal wolfdogs that chased runaways or ate the offspring of the slaves. The wolfdogs were given to the witches of America by the indigenous people from the north. They were specifically bred to guard and protect the witches from their enemies, especially the Christian defilement of the Inquisition.

Torture was a common pastime for these witch handlers. Screams echoed throughout the fields. Young men were perfect targets for these hags. Pino would hear stories of a young man who was forced to dress as a woman and was controlled like a puppet to perform foolish and humiliating dances, or reenact scenes of fairies and princesses, and other foolish American fairy tales. Pino would often hear of handlers manipulating young men by offering them to come inside their nice cottages, offer them better food and a bed, but at a very fine cost. They would then force them to have sex in return. One would think that a man would most likely not refuse such an offer–sex for a better life? The victim would often agree. Then the men would then be forced onto their hands and knees and the rest was left for the poor man to tell the tale.

Those who did live to tell the tale were often promoted. These men were enforcers. The enforcers were chosen specifically for their good behavior and their willingness to obey their handlers and the camp. As a sign of their good will, they were castrated and forced to wear a yellow sash. They were often seen beating the other slaves to work harder and faster.

Whenever they would turn away from the slaves, the workers would then raise two fingers in the shape of a "V" as an offensive sign to the enforcer. They were traitors and not to be trusted.

The day then turned into night. A bovine horn was blasted from across the fields signifying that the day of work was finished. The slaves groaned and marched in unison towards the center of camp. On their backs was all the corn they had collected from the afternoon to the evening. The slaves trudged and limped in exhaustion after a long day of working under the beating sun. A young woman collapsed behind Pino. He saw her collapse, but he had to keep moving. A handler zoomed past Pino. The horse panted and whinnied. He heard the cries of the woman as she was beaten mercilessly to stand. The line trailed around her like a row of ants moving around a fallen leaf as they brought food to their queen. At the end of the row, Pino presented his bag to the handler. She inspected the bag and gave a nod of approval and instructed him to put it into the wagon, where it would be distributed throughout the continent.

Pino rubbed his aching shoulders and back. He then joined the crowd of workers that circled around the center of the camp. In the center, three metal poles stood valiantly to the crowd. Chained to the poles were three slaves that were chosen at random for the daily torturing. The enforcers then stood behind three slaves and whipped them until their backs were raw. The screams of the tortured echoed throughout the valley. The camps made the prisoners watch this cruel randomness in order to show dominance over the poor workers. Pino was thankful that there were no children working the fields; instead, they were sent to the learning camps to "re-evaluate" their Christian ways, but the babies were sent to the markets. The witches wanted to send a message. They wanted their prisoners to fear the potential of their great nation. They wanted them to fear the mighty fist of the Horned Father. He was the enforcer, and the witches were his instruments. There was no hope in these camps.

Pino's back burned as he watched the whip crack the flesh of the tortured. In the beginning of his imprisonment at the work camp, Pino was often whipped and tortured. He saw the blood splatter as it fed the dusty earth. He constantly defied the handlers and would often be strangled, hung, drowned, and whipped for his supposed insolence. As more blood was drawn and more scars healed his back, he became silent. He would often go days without saying a word. Whenever he spoke to answer the handler, his voice sounded alien and strange. He did not know who he was. He was no one.

Pino's back ached as he trudged back to his small cottage with his housemates. They groaned and buckled as they plopped onto the bottom bunk. Inside were three bunks. In the center of the cottage was a small hearth that kept the men warm for the remainder of the evening. They took out the last remaining pieces of their daily rations and scarfed them viciously as they lay in their beds. The rations consisted of moldy stale bread and rusted water. Pino took a bite of his bread, but maggots sprouted from his bite. Pino took out the maggots one by one and dropped them on the ground and continued to feverishly eat his meal.

Pino then got out a nail from underneath his pillow that he kept secretly. On the top of his bunk, he scratched a tally on it. He counted 130 days. This was remarkable considering that most prisoners only lasted a few weeks. Pino was one of the few hardy workers within the camp. In a fit of inspiration and a desire to break the routine, he then carved a tau τ. Pino folded his hands in prayer and bowed in reverence to the tiny symbol he just carved. For the first time in ages, he began to pray.

"Lord," he quietly prayed to himself. "Please protect my dear Arturo as we embark on this perilous path you have sent us. It is your will to help us and protect. It is your will to allow me to see him again and to allow the both of us to continue–"

Pino then stopped for a moment. He heard the cicadas and grasshoppers begin their nightly serenade. He continued on.

"Please help me escape this wretched place so I can see my brother and tell him how sorry I am. I was foolish. I was foolish for being disrespectful to the Salemite court. I only wanted to protect his honor, Father. I wanted to kill them. Father, I wanted to kill them all."

Pino closed his eyes and he heard gunshots and screams of women and children. Images of bloodshed and murder flashed before his eyes. He tossed and turned in his bed, trying to shoo away the horrendous images of warfare. He pictured himself and his Samuelite comrades marching the streets of Tokyo. They marched in unison with their big black boots, their gray and red uniforms, glimmering in the sun. He then heard the screams of hundreds of women and children as he witnessed enormous flames engulfing the Japanese markets. He saw an abandoned Buddhist temple collapse as it was blown into a pile of rubble. The secret Buddhists scurried out of the burning pavilion, trying to escape the Inquisitional enforcements. Pino stood on the throat of a Buddhist priest and laughed. The priest begged for mercy in his foreign tongue. Pino only laughed until the priest's final breath was expelled.

The scene then shifted to Pino standing with a line of broad-chested barbarians who wore long furs and hats made from animal hide. They were shackled, brought to their knees, and presented to the Samuelite captain of Tokyo. His words sounded muffled, but Pino heard the other officers laugh as they brandished their knives in unison and slit the throats of the Japanese barbarians. Behind them, the cathedral of Tokyo burned. Hellfire was at hand. It consumed the beautiful building.

The image changed again, and bloodied pieces of silver were poured into his hands. He pictured riding on horseback and hunting down various outlaws. He was a mercenary again, hunting down strange individuals in strange lands. He crossed various oceans, walked strange grasslands, and felt the beating sun of the desert. He killed one after the other after the other. The hellfire of blood and torture consumed Pino. Tears streamed down his face as he rolled and shook in fear.

Pino shook his head and his vision turned to black. He took a deep breath. An image of Johannesburg came to him. Pino had returned to South Africa. With him was his smiling mustached brother, Arturo. Together they were building a house alongside his other Traveler brothers. He was then teaching the young children of Johannesburg how to play bocce. They giggled and laughed as he chased them when they successfully knocked his ball away from the smaller ball. Then he and Arturo performed silly biblical performances in front of the village. He dressed as Bathsheba and Arturo was King David. Pino then began to scandalously dance as he pretended to wash himself with a giant washing brush. The people of the village laughed and chuckled. The crowd loved them. Arturo would break character and laugh at Pino's ridiculous performance. He then pictured the laughter of Arturo as he brought water to the children of Johannesburg. Hope and happiness filled Pino. He felt a small flame of warmth spread from his belly and enter his heart. Pino wiped his tears and continued his prayer.

"Lord, please help me escape this place. My life is in your hands. I ask you to make me an instrument of peace. *Benedictus pacis*. Amen."

Pino unfolded his hands and closed his eyes. Thoughts and ideas of a plan to escape flooded Pino's mind as he drifted off to sleep. He dreamed peacefully for the first time. Hope was finally near.

14

The raven circled the bleak, clear gray sky shrouded Salem. The markets buzzed and chattered with life. Salemites bartered and haggled for goods and items that came from throughout the vast American continent. Children mischievously ran the streets, pickpocketing ancient men with tree branches for canes and pulling the tails of street cats and dogs. Traffic flooded the streets. Hundreds of buggies and carriages fumed with impatience as Arturo walked along the narrow cobble-stoned sidewalks. He had to be quick because he had to go to class in the afternoon.

Arturo scoured each tent, tentatively looking for the items on his shopping list. Arturo was still getting used to the urban setting. Not only was Salem so large, but the tents' locations were never consistent. Every day, they would change and move street to street or sometimes completely disappear altogether. Finding these tents made it frustrating for Arturo. It made it harder to accept this strange continent because of its strange ways.

Arturo hated asking other people because they would immediately know he was an outsider, and he would immediately be mistrusted. Although Salem was a place of freedom and ideals, they easily put up walls against the help of a stranger. They knew he was not one of them. Arturo would try his best to speak English, but it was always very poor. He would often ask Orla to help dress him like a true Salemite, but he would always stick out like an orange in an apple barrel. People would give him strange stares and stand clear from his walking path. Yet, Arturo was determined to assimilate the best he could.

Arturo finally found the tent that carried all the supplies that he needed: a journal, quills, ink, and pencils. He wanted another journal in order to make blueprints to keep his mind busy and at ease. He missed inventing. His hands would often shake uncontrollably if he saw a piece of metal or saw the rolling of a carriage or buggy. He would sometimes spend the afternoon watching the local blacksmith and engineers make and design carriages, buggies, and all metal works. Often, he would go to the local sweet shop, grab a sweet and spend hours watching through the window the exquisite metal work. His mustache would twitch in delight as he smelled burning oil as the buggies passed by. It intoxicated Arturo. However, he forbade himself from inventing whatsoever. He knew that such skill would make him noticed by the Salemites.

Arturo was never allowed to wander off too far into the city of Salem. Calciph followed closely at his heels. Arturo had no friends as he walked the streets of Salem. He had no companion but this old grizzled black cat by his side. Arturo would sometimes even talk to Calciph and have conversations with him. The old cat would only listen and walk closely to Arturo, probably ignoring him.

Arturo approached the tent with his money carefully counted and ready.

"How much journal ink?" asked Arturo with his poor English.

"*Twenty shillings*," said the old witch at the counter, suspiciously eyeing Arturo.

"By God, the prices have gotten ridiculous," Arturo remarked to Calciph, as the old cat licked himself. "*I pay ten.*"

"*I will give it to you for fifteen, foreigner*," said the old witch, crossing her arms in a fit of stubbornness.

"*Deal*," agreed Arturo in a sigh of annoyance. Arturo then gave the old witch her fifteen shillings and put his supplies away in his duffle bag that Orla had made for him. The bag was bright purple with a golden rope. It was soft and sleek to the touch. Pedestrians walked past Arturo and bumped into him in an urgent frenzy. The buggies continued to honk, as the horses bucked nervously from the chaotic noise.

"Wow, Calciph," exclaimed Arturo. "Look how crazy the city is around here. I wonder why there is so much traffic."

"'Beats me, Doc'," said Arturo, throwing in Calciph's voice as a response to his statement. "'I wonder what all the commotion is all about...'"

"I'll say! We are approaching a full moon I think."

"'Well, I hope everything will be ok, old boy. I am always here to protect you.'"

"Thank you, Calciph. You're a good ol' chump."

Arturo laughed at himself. Never in his wildest days would he even have seen himself talk to a cat, let alone be part of a Devil worshiping society. Back home, he would have been seen as the crazy man in Cassino. Arturo recalled taking his wife and children to the Italian countryside, where his own father would take him in the summers with Roberto. There, his family had a ranch where they kept animals of all shapes and sizes– from chickens to goats, to ducks to horses. Arturo would take his children to the stables and move the horse's lips and give the horse a silly voice. His children would scream and giggle in excitement. Arturo looked at the scraggly Calciph and sighed.

HONK!!! HONK!!! HONK!!!

Arturo turned towards the street and saw a small truck had completely stopped in the middle of the road. The driver was an old man. He slowly got out of his vehicle to investigate. A trail of steam trickled from the sides of the hood and into the atmosphere. The man lifted the hood and scratched his beard nervously. Drivers behind him honked and yelled viciously, urging the man to move out of the way. A man with a herd of camels shook his fist and cursed at the old man. The old man continued scratching his beard and looked confused and bewildered by the chaos.

Arturo quickly walked towards the old man. He was possibly in his 80s, had remnants of wispy white hair on top of his head and a scraggly beard. He wore a simple brown sack for his cloak, sandals, and large specs that magnified his eyes three times their original size. He smelled of manure and was completely covered in feathers. The man shook his head, completely overwhelmed, not knowing what to do. The old man cried,

"I am sorry, young man. My truck began to sputter and cough. It then sputtered again and then she died all together. I

can't be late! I have an important delivery to make! I will lose

everything!"

Arturo then looked at the back of the truck and it was full of birds inside their cages. They were birds of all shapes, sizes, and species. Arturo saw blue jays, flamingos, penguins, falcons, emus, and hummingbirds. They all chirped and squawked and tweeted frantically. Arturo put a calming hand on the old man's shoulder.

"*It ok, man,*" stumbled Arturo in his poor English. "*I fix now. Ok?*"

The old man sighed in relief. Arturo then saw the blacksmith. The blacksmith had completely stopped his work and watched the commotion. Arturo pointed to the blacksmith's tools. The blacksmith chuckled. A wave of trust and comradery connected the two. The blacksmith took off his own apron and tool belt and gave it to Arturo. With his sweaty rough hands, he gave Arturo a pat on the shoulder of encouragement. Arturo smiled and nodded in thanks. Arturo then turned towards the engine. Immediately, his mustache began to twitch. He was ready to work.

A crowd began to surround Arturo as he worked his divine magic. Arturo peeked under the hood. A sudden sense of euphoria overwhelmed Arturo. His body seemed to have lifted from the ground. Arturo's hands felt as if God had entered him and guided him to every correct area of work throughout the engine. Arturo saw that the engine's cylinder was completely cooked. The engine leaked and sputtered as heat and smoke filled the air. Arturo then grabbed a piece of hard metal, carved it, and created a new and improved cylinder for the engine. He then urged the old man to start the truck. The engine roared with life!

The crowd cheered and praised. A wave of relief washed over Arturo. The old man approached Arturo, shaking his hand with a surprisingly firm grip.

"Thank you, young man," said the old man. *"You may be a foreigner but you sure as hell know how to work your way around a buggy! How can I ever repay you?"*

173

"*No, thank you!*" Arturo said sheepishly.

The old man went around the back of the truck and gave Arturo a small bird cage with a little bird singing inside it. Arturo was astonished. He looked inside. The bird was a beautiful little thing, with blue and white feathers, a short beak, but lovely sharp wings. It sang to Arturo as he observed the precious creature.

"*Beautiful, what kind?*" Arturo said curiously, feeling more confident with his English.

"*This here is a swallow!*" said the old man proudly. "*They are pretty little things. They sing pretty songs in the morning. They are normally used for sacrifices, but I never like that idea. She is all yours. Thank you again, sire.*"

Arturo thanked the man again for his precious reward and nodded to Calciph that he was ready to walk home. Arturo felt fulfilled. He felt fulfilled that he made a difference. In this godless land, Arturo was making a difference. Perhaps the people of Salem were not as evil as the Inquisition had taught him. Perhaps his entire life has been a lie, a ploy of political

174

deceit. Yes, the people of America were barbaric in their customs, yet so were the Inquisition. Perhaps he could continue his vow as a Traveler but in a different way. Perhaps he could establish himself within Salem, find Pino, and free him from bondage. The two brothers would finally be free.

Arturo walked home with a skip and a jig. He was overwhelmed with joy. He observed his little bird and whispered to it. He prayed to it saying how beautiful her feathers were. She fluttered in the cage, trying to escape. She chirped in frustration and continued fluttering around. Eventually, she finally gave up and perched in exhaustion. Arturo looked at his little friend again and his heart sank for a moment. An idea came to him.

Arturo walked behind the house and entered the Adamson Garden. There, a proud oak tree blew into the autumn breeze. The leaves fell gently onto Arturo as he looked at his little friend. He sat by a nearby bench and enjoyed the beauty and nature. He then looked at his little bird friend one last time. He opened her cage. She flew away and perched on a nearby tree. She sang a song in thanks. The bird flew away into the gray sky. Arturo watched until she became only a small dot and disappeared. Arturo hoped that one day he, too, could be a bird. One day.

15

The night was alive in the camps of Carolina. The wolfdogs howled and moaned in hunger. The horned owl screeched in assertion. The wind blew and bellowed, allowing the nearby trees to groan. The sky was pitch black, only showing a glimmer of the full moon. Thunder bellowed in the distance, but there was not a cloud or star in sight. Darkness consumed the night sky. The shadows danced in the cornfields. All was restless that evening, especially the mischievous Pino.

Pino waited beside his window, holding a sack tightly to his chest. His stomach grumbled, begging for him to eat his daily rations of moldy bread. Pino clutched his stomach, quietly begging for it to stop its rant. Pino had been saving his food rations for about a week. His eyes grew weary not only with exhaustion, but hunger. He only sustained himself with the rusted water and by eating tufts of grass that grew under the cabin. The taste of earth was still present in his mouth. He smacked his lips to get rid of the taste, yet it remained. Pino had to be alert. Pino had to stay focused.

"Hey, Blondie," said one of the bunkmates. "How come you're not eating?"

The bunkmate was tall, skinny, and had a long-hooked nose. He was completely bald, had a scruffed face and deep blue eyes. He had a few scars on his chest and a brand on his chest of a holy cross. He looked exhausted and malnourished, yet he had a deep voice. He had only been here for a month. This was the first conversation Pino was having with his bunkmates.

"I am not hungry," Pino whispered sternly, keeping his bread close to him, still looking out the window.

"Not hungry, huh?" said the bunkmate in a louder voice. His friends stopped and looked at him and Pino. Pino hated drawing attention to himself, especially in front of these brutes. They all looked tough and worn. They were all tall and muscular in stature. They all had a strange look in their eyes. They had the eyes of war.

"No, I am not hungry." Pino said angrily. "Got a problem with that, old boy? Piss off will ya?"

"Listen, no need for theatrics. I know a man who's trying to escape when I see one. No sane man would hoard food in a place like this unless they are saving it for later someplace else."

Pino gave the bunkmate a look of guilt and furrowed his eyebrows and looked towards the window.

"Blondie, I promise I won't rat you out to the enforcer-fucks out there. Unless…"

"Unless what?" Pino said curiously.

"Unless you have me and my friends join you in your little escape."

"You might as well rot here if that is the case, friend. If you wanna escape, by all means take this bag here of my rations and go off your merry way. As a group it'll be nearly impossible. I am doing this alone."

The other bunkmates circled Pino. They tightened their circle and glared at Pino as he sat in his bed, completely outnumbered. The smell of the brutes entered Pino's nose. They smelled of earth, sweat and manure. They reeked. The skinny bunkmate chuckled to himself.

"Brother, I can assure you that we are more than qualified to handle an escape like this one," chuckled the skinny bunkmate. "We may look like a bundle of bone heads, but we are full blown Inquisition. We are former HOWs, Blondie. We are mean and we are sure as hell qualified."

Pino sat astonished.

"We heard about that squabble back in Japan and your mercenary work. I guess the rumors are true. I gotta say, my boys and I, we admire a ruthless killer. You get the job done, get away with it, and disappear. You're basically like us but better. And in all honesty, we couldn't give a flying shit about the Inquisition. We just wanna go home."

The bunkmate reached out his hand as a sign of friendship. Pino took it and shook it with a small smile on his face. The other gentlemen began to chuckle and patted each other for the new formation of their friendship.

"What do they call you, brother?" said Pino, shaking his new comrade's hand.

"They call me Paolo. This is Raul, Gregor, Giovanni, and of course Toto. They are my mates."

"I'm Pino Alessandro. Gentlemen, tonight we will plan and prepare for tomorrow. And tomorrow at sundown when the moon is full and bright, we finally escape this rotting hell hole. Tomorrow we will walk home free boys."

***

The orange sun began to set. The shadows of the crops began to grow as the sun slowly disappeared across the endless fields of the camp. The crickets sang their nightly songs and the snores of thousands of clunky cottages were heard. Everyone was asleep after a long day's work of picking, packing and cropping. The only cottage that stood awake was that of Pino and his fellow prisoners.

The majority of the evening before consisted of preparation for tonight's escape. They had to be quick and diligent with their planning. Pino gathered with his new comrades. They needed to be alert from not only the witches but the enforcers. They had to arm themselves, but this was proving difficult. They were naked, unarmed prisoners with only their thumbs to twiddle. They only had small two-inch knives that were used to cut down crops. Pino suggested the brilliant idea of using the legs of their wooden bunk beds and sharpening them to create make-shift weapons. The gang grunted in agreement.

Pino had never been great with handiwork, especially when it came to carpentry or any arts and crafts. He whittled his piece of wood but struggled with his small knife. The wood was hard, rough, and chipped. Pino winced in pain as splinters entered his palms and fingers. He imagined his dear brother, Arturo, flawlessly whittling his weapon. "*Practice makes perfect,*" Pino thought to himself. Within two hours, Pino had successfully made a spear. It was around four and a half feet long, light to hold, and incredibly smooth.

After hours of preparation, Pino and the prison gang were ready for battle. Pino looked out the window and saw the fainting hours of the evening come to fruition. The sky turned from blue to orange, and then from orange to black. The moon rose high in the cloudless night. No cricket songs. No coyotes howled to the moon. No snores in the cottages. The night was quiet and still.

"Gentlemen, remember: eyes on the sky and on the ground. We take out anything that moves. And use your weapons sparingly."

The men nodded in agreement, holding their newly made spears ready for action. Pino waited outside observing the lingering watchtower in the distance. For a few moments they waited for the lanterns to turn on as the watchers surveyed the area. The blinding light scoured cottage to cottage, hoping for a prisoner to attempt to break their curfew or escape the camp. They waited for the light to pass their cottage. Pino and the gang then jumped from the cottage window.

The group split up and hid behind each cottage. Silence still clung to the air. The dirt ground crunched loudly after each footstep. The group then resorted to taking off their sandals and walking barefoot. The pebbles and soil pierced and poked their bare feet, but they had to continue. Pino looked to the sky with his trusty spear at hand, scanning the ground every few moments and then intently watching the sky. He saw some movement in the dark night sky. He raised his fist and the men stopped moving.

A single dot was seen floating in the sky. It sailed slowly through the dark night sky. The dot projected the shape of a dainty female figure into the moonlight. Pino looked closer and observed the girl as she flew overhead, surveying the camp. The witch completely naked and was covered in bright red blood over her milky white skin. She had dark hair, was very petite, and flew on a rickety broom like a small bird. The men had to be cautious.

Pino motioned to the gang to remain silent. He then stood from his crouching position and blended with the shadows.

He held his spear, pointed at his young target. He took a few deep breaths for a few moments. A mask of concentration was on Pino's face. There was no room for error. He had only one chance and one chance only. He closed his eyes and thought of his training. He was focused. He was calm. He felt as if he were riding the waves of the ocean. He was in control. He was the spear. He was the earth. He was the hunter. Pino opened his eyes and threw the spear. The spear pierced through the atmosphere like a bullet and shot the young witch square in the chest. Without a moment to scream or cry out, she fell loosely off her broom and onto the soft ground in the fields. Pino pointed forward and the men continued on.

The men made it past the camp's village and ran through the fields. Pino motioned for them to scatter and meet at the edge of the camp. They had to be as quick and as swift as possible. Like scythes, they sliced through the tall stalks of corn, running for their lives. Pino ran as quickly as he could. Blindly, he ran forward making his own path. Because the corn was so tall, Pino was unable to see anything that was in front of him. He continued running forward. Pino was soon becoming dizzy and seeing strange shapes. It had been a while since he had endured such urgency. He had to continue forward.

A howl was heard in the distance. The men stopped and waited. Another howl was heard. The men heard panting and barking behind them.

"Run!" whispered Pino to his men. They sprinted forward. The voices of women shouting in the sky were heard. Pino heard a few screams in the distance, gurgles, and then complete silence. Pino heard more cries of pain and torture behind him, but he urged himself to continue forward.

Pino then saw the edge of the camp. It was an incredible wall of cobblestone that was chipped, ancient, and riddled in moss and leafy vines. The great wall was approximately twenty feet tall. It was almost green due to the vegetation and wild weeds grew around it. The wall was neglected but still posed as a chance of opportunity. Pino had no chance to observe whether the stones were trustworthy enough to climb. He had to move. Howls and growls were heard in the distance behind him. Pino sparked an idea! He grabbed the strong vines and began climbing them with great ease. He climbed and climbed the mighty wall. Freedom was close. Very close.

Pino climbed up the wall and saw the wolf dogs bark and growl viciously as he reached the top. Pino looked at their wicked sharp fangs glaring at him, demanding that he come down so they could rip him to shreds. Their eyes glowed green in the darkness. Pino, drenched in sweat, took a few deep breaths. The dogs howled once more.

Pino climbed down the massive wall. He heard the screams in the air. The screams made his stomach lurch in fear, but he had to run. He ran through the heavy brush. Thickets and thorns pierced his skin as he sprinted through the forest like a rabbit escaping from its predator. He winced in pain but sped on. Pino could taste blood on his lips from the thorns. Fear consumed him. He felt the claws of his captors coming close as the wind whizzed past his ears.

"Brother!" shouted Paolo from the back of the brush. "Please help us!"

Pino then heard a grunting sound and a simple thud. Paolo was dead. He couldn't turn back to help his comrades. He had to keep moving. Howls and cries hung in the air like a noose. They swayed and rang in Pino's ears. He turned back to see if the wolves were chasing him.

THUD!

A gigantic tree appeared before Pino. He stopped and observed the tree for a moment and saw it was hollow. Pino then burrowed inside the tree and waited for a sound to pass by. Silence returned to the forest. The wind stopped, as did the howling. The witches ceased their screams and yowls. Pino waited for a moment and looked through a small crevice within the tree. He saw a group of wolves followed by a group of enforcers. The wolves sniffed, their long snouts salivating with interest and hunger. They barked and ran off in the distance away from the tree. Pino sighed in relief.

Pino felt a gust of hot air blow against the back of his neck. He froze. Pino wasn't alone. Something was in the tree. A dark figure growled behind him. Pino slowly turned. Pino saw ugly yellow fangs from the beast. The big snout was long and wet. Its eyes glowed yellow in the dark hollow tree. The eyes possessed no soul. The beast was covered with its ferociously long matted fur. The beast's hot stench reached Pino's nostrils. Pino was paralyzed in fright. It was one of the guard wolves. Pino had been caught.

Pino slowly walked out of the tree and lifted his hands in surrender. The vicious beast growled and cornered him against the tree. Pino then sheathed his dagger. The small, yet wicked blade shined in the moonlight. He had to face the beast before he could face the others. He had never killed an animal before. This would be a first for the young Traveler.

"Come on, you son of a bitch!" angrily whispered Pino wielding his knife, as the wolf snapped at him. "Let's dance, you furry mutt."

Before the wolf was ready to pounce, Pino felt his body lift into the air, and he was thrown against the tree. Pino's eyes blurred. He saw only shadows and stars. Pino wobbled and fumbled as he tried to regain himself. He saw a pale figure approach him. With long, clawed hands, it took him by the neck and pinned him to the tree. Pino's vision finally cleared. Lo and behold it was his captors.

Ten witches approached the tree on horseback. Their horses buckled and neighed in stress as the witches held them by the hair and kicked their sides to regain their majestic composure. Each one of them held a torch in one hand and a scythe on their backs. They sat naked on their loyal steeds and laughed as Pino weakly hung onto the tree by one of the guards. A deep gallop was heard from the distance. It was the warden.

Warden Williams rode a steed of great majesty. The horse was twice the size of the other horses, with an incredibly long mane, snout, and gave a deep whinny as it clunked its massive hooves to the forest floor. Beside her, hanging loosely from a belt around the horse, were the heads of Paolo and his gang members. Like medals, they gleamed brightly in the forest as the warden's horse pranced around the brush. Williams wore her hair in a tight bun and her eyes glowed green in the dark forest. She smiled her usual wicked smile. She had been waiting for a night like this. She had been waiting for a special occasion to torture someone–especially an escapee like Pino.

"Isn't this adorable, girls?" laughed Williams. *"These animals don't seem to like their new home. I try to make it as comfortable as possible for you, little shits. Yet, you have the audacity to try and escape."*

The other witches laughed and cackled. They knew what would come next after the warden's little charade.

"And we all know what happens to our pets who try to leave my camp. Don't we, you little shit?"

Pino spat at her feet. The other witches cackled in delight, as did Williams. Williams held out her hand lazily as she laughed at Pino. The witch then let go of Pino. He coughed and hacked. The witch gave Williams a small white object. It was a small doll that was all white, faceless, and completely plain. However, a strand of hair was wrapped completely around its neck. Without a moment's notice, the warden violently twisted the doll's arm. A surge of pain erupted in Pino's arm. His arm twisted and turned, alongside the doll's. Pino screamed in agony and knelt to the ground in pain.

"Please no more," begged Pino hoarsely. "Please."

The warden laughed, as did her posse. The warden held her torch towards the doll's head. The flames gently caressed the doll's head. Pino screamed again, holding his hand. He rolled around on the ground. He felt as if he had plunged his head into an open bonfire. He rolled and moaned and screamed in agony. They continued to laugh and cry out into the moonlight. The warden looked down at Pino in satisfaction.

"Just kill me already, warden," shouted Pino, the flames still engulfing him, cooking his brain to a roast. "Please kill me."

Williams gave a good hearty laugh and removed the flames from the doll's head. Instant coolness filled Pino's cranium. Pino took a few long deep breaths and collapsed to the ground. His eyes rolled to the back of his head. He was still awake, but the forest began to spin. The warden then turned the doll to its hands and knees. Pino did the same as the doll. Like an animal, the naked Pino knelt before the witches, exposing every

192

inch of himself to the group of women. He groaned in embarrassment and delirium.

Williams dramatically pulled a long, pointed, iron rod at her fellow sisters. They cheered and cackled in delight.

"You know what happens when someone tries to escape this camp?" asked the warden, playfully. *"They get a nice long metal rod up their ass till you like it."*

Williams then grabbed Pino by the ear and prepared the rod for Pino. Pino screamed, but he couldn't move his body. He was trapped. Pino closed his eyes and awaited his torture. He prayed for forgiveness. He prayed for Arturo and his freedom. This was the end.

Williams then stopped and dropped her rod to the ground. It cluttered as it met with the forest floor. Pino sighed with relief. Williams's eyes widened. She pulled his ear again and observed it.

"Well I'll be damned. Ladies, looks like this one is getting out of this shit hole alive. Prepare a truck for an overnight drive. We gotta send this one to Salem."

16

The laughter and screams of children filled the halls of the Metropolitan School of Salem. Hundreds of children both young and old were herded into their classrooms as they prepared for their teacher to begin class. They sang songs and nursery rhymes of their forefathers, they doodled in their notebooks, and made makeshift dolls from twigs and small trinkets. Children were a rarity within Salem, yet they were treasured and revered by society. They were the future. They were meant to ensure the legacy of America. The legacy of the Horned Father.

Arturo was excelling in school. He had received high marks and was constantly improving. Arturo excelled in American history, literature, mathematics, and more. His favorite subject was art because it allowed him to freely express himself, but he had to keep the meanings and symbolism behind his work private. In the beginning, Arturo had a hard time being in the classroom, mostly because he was moved to a class full of six and seven-year-old children.

The instructor was no help at all when she addressed how a grown man was sitting in their class, especially in a desk far too small for his comfort. The children would throw wads of paper at him as he attempted to listen to the teacher during her lecture. At recess, the children were merciless. They would point at Arturo and call him "Boogeyman" or "Beanstalk" because he would hunch over the children as he awkwardly walked past the screaming children like a monster. The children would laugh and point at him as he sat awkwardly, trying to complete his Social Studies worksheet. However, Arturo was determined to prove to not only his classmates but the entire school that he would not be the court jester.

The following day, the usual classroom antics continued. A hurricane of paper and other materials soared through the air and ricocheted from the towering Arturo. Instead of throwing them away, Arturo kept the small wads of papers. He scavenged and hoarded them like a dragon on a mountain of gold and silver.

The children grew curious, distracted by Arturo's strange behavior. Usually, he would try and swat the small wads of paper, but today was different. Arturo's mustache began to twitch. He looked at the wads and he began to work. The children, at this point, completely ignored the teacher who was explaining the geography of the Province of the Raven. A few moments passed by and there was silence that clung in the air.

Suddenly, Arturo flew his hand in the air and a fleet of paper aeroplanes were released into the air. They all landed on top of the children, sailing in all directions. The children screamed and giggled in delight. The children got up from their desks and ran around the classroom chasing them. The teacher barked at her students to sit down but they wouldn't listen. She turned and found a laughing Arturo who sat in his abnormally small desk. However, her scolding turned into a smile as the children ran up to Arturo and gave him hugs, begging him to teach them how to make his paper aeroplanes.

In no time, Arturo became the most popular student in the school. He was not only known for his paper aeroplanes, but also his strange yet fascinating tricks and creations. He taught the students how to fold paper into various shapes, like animals and other everyday objects. He would also teach the children how to sketch and bring life into the pages of their books. He quickly jumped from grade level to grade level in a matter of weeks. By September, he was in a classroom full of young adult students who were prepared for the real world the following year. He met all Lady Cathleen's academic expectations and anticipated to finish his education required by law by the end of November.

Despite his near completion of his accelerated education, Arturo enjoyed the classroom and wanted to learn more. He wanted to learn more about these strange people and their strange land and culture. It was unlike any other. Yes, they were savages, but they were so vastly different from Inquisitional Europe. Arturo was a ghost who observed the strange land in infinite wonder. Arturo would return to school midday, do some grocery shopping, or stroll around the market in the morning, and study at home. He developed a routine.

Today, in celebration, the instructor was telling the story of the first Devil's Sabbath. She skidded across the classroom excitedly as she pointed at the archival photos of grossly illustrated Catholic missionaries as they menacingly encircled over a group of witches that shined expressions of innocence on their faces as they burned to a crisp in an open bonfire.

"The Spanish missionaries and the Puritans, my children, are the very reason why we are here today," said the teacher proudly to the class. The students seemed completely disinterested as half of them snored at their desks as the midday sun peeked through the windows. However, the instructor continued.

"The Spanish Inquisition failed to convert our forefathers by stripping them of their humanity and they were burned alive at the stake. Our forefathers retaliated! How did our forefathers retaliate?"

The instructor paused for a moment urgently waiting for a student to raise their hand. Arturo looked around the room. A young witch had her head down and had left a puddle of drool as

199

she snoozed into her desk. Arturo smirked at the sight and then raised his hand.

"*The forefathers killed both the Spanish and Puritan children,*" said Arturo. "*The purge started in Salem and then continued through the rest of the colonies. It was meant to be an act of justice.*"

"*Very good, Arturo!*" said the instructor excitedly. Arturo sat proud of himself, beaming for perfectly answering the teacher's question in English. "*That is exactly what happened. We must also remember this day was specifically chosen because it is the same day that Adam and Eve were tempted by the Horned Father to eat from the Tree of Knowledge. It is important to know that it was the will of the Horned Father that allowed our forefathers to rightfully purge this land so that we can obtain this beautiful and bountiful nation that we share with our indigenous allies in the north and the south!*"

A student in the back raised their hand. He was a small boy with ratty features, spectacled, and waved his hand in the air desperately to get his teacher's attention.

"Yes, Archie?" asked the instructor.

"You talk about the will of the Horned Father. Why won't you tell us about the Man of the Fields and the prophecy? Is the new prophecy the will of the Father?"

"Well, Archie, I am afraid that I can't answer that question because..." the teacher hesitated as she thought to give him a concrete answer. *"It is not part of the curriculum. Something like that is meant to be discussed when you are all much older. Let's move on."*

"But we will be older by the end of this fall!" said a female student near the window. *"We are old enough to understand!"*

The children shouted in agreement. They began whispering and gossiping amongst each other as the flabbergasted teacher tried to regain control of the class. Arturo sat silently in the center front row as the chaos ensued. He simply looked at the teacher as she scrambled for control. He did not want to cause more tension between the students and teacher.

"We demand to know!"

"Is this the end of us all?"

"Are we all going to die?"

"ENOUGH!" boomed the teacher in frustration as she slammed her fist on her desk. Instantly the children became silent. The teacher then took a deep breath, straightened her hair, and composed herself. "Class, I will say that the prophecy is indeed true. However, it will most likely happen long after you are all gone. The prophecy never clearly specified when it would come to fruition. It can be today, tomorrow or a thousand years from now! I can recall the Prophecy of 1907 that said the children of Salem would one day starve in five moons! And guess what: all the children of Salem are well fed and happy!"

"Yes, that's true," said Archie. *"But that is also false. It depends on how you look at the meaning of starve. Maybe the prophecy wasn't implying hunger in terms of food but instead something else. There has been a shortage of infants, meaning that they are low in supplies of baby blood and teeth which is a necessity for our people. People are no longer keeping infants*

alive because of this thirst for their blood, making it a non-renewable resource. Infant blood was once as bountiful as water but now it has become super, super rare! The prices of infant blood have tripled over the past five years. Demand is only getting higher, and the blood of infants is now only being saved for the elite members of Salem."

"Yes, Archie. But..."

"Also, the people of Salem have been showing signs of being barren or their children being stillborn. There will be no more future generations of witches. Will this be the end of our people? Is this the will of the Horned Father, instructor?"

Before the teacher would answer, the school bell rang above them, ending the day. The teacher gave a sigh of relief and dismissed the students for the day. The children chatted and gossiped amongst themselves about the previous events. Arturo put his pencil behind his ear, gathered his books and headed to the door.

BAM! BAM! BAM!

Arturo froze. The students in the classroom screamed in fright. The instructor slammed the classroom door and locked it. Her mouth gaped open in absolute horror as she stood in front of the door. The students all ran to the corner as Arturo remained by his desk. Gunshots and shouting were heard outside of the door!

"DEUS VULT!" shouted a male voice from the hallway. Gunshots continued as the children cowered in fear, covering their ears. Arturo's heart began to race. Was this it? Was it the Inquisition and were they here to finally rescue him?

Arturo peeked through the classroom door's tiny window. There, he saw a group of raggedy dressed men scouring the hallways with automatic machine guns at hand. They were tall, brutish and all possessed a Christian cross, branded on their necks. They slammed into the doors of other classrooms. The students screamed in horror as the man mercilessly shot inside the classroom. The air was then filled with silence when the shooting ceased. Thoughts of escape raced in Arturo's mind. A thought struck Arturo like lightning…little Rosie! He had to save little Rosie.

The children clung to the other side of the classroom creating a barrier of desks between the classroom door. The children cried and screamed and begged for the Horned Father to save them from this chaos. Arturo gazed upon his fellow classmates. Innocence radiated from the young witches like the rising morning sun. The golden sun almost created little halos that shined on top of their heads through the window. Arturo's mustache began to twitch!

Arturo grabbed the nearest chair from the desk and broke the window. The children screamed as the glass shattered and fell onto the classroom floor.

"Everyone!" anxiously shouted Arturo. *"Climb out the window! I'll distract the men outside. Call the authorities!"*

The children then climbed out of the window one by one, running home and disappearing into the city. Arturo looked out the window and saw a crowd surrounding the school entrance, eager to see all the commotion. The crowd shouted and cried out for their children as the rounds of gunfire continued. Arturo's adrenaline kicked in. He had to save little Rosie.

Rosie's classroom was at the end of the hallway. Arturo opened the door slightly and saw an armed man trying to kick the door open. The man was tall, bald, and wore ragged brown robes. He tightly held his gun as he tried to kick the door down with his heavy iron boots. He grunted, spat, and swore as he kicked the door. The children inside the classroom screamed in terror. Arturo had to be careful. He had no weapon and was alone. Arturo slowly poked his head out of the classroom. The armed man was alone in the hallway.

Arturo slowly opened the door and snuck his way across the hallway. He tiptoed cautiously as the violent man repeatedly kicked the door. Arturo slowly removed his scarf. Quick as a flash, Arturo wrapped the scarf around the man. The man fought and kicked violently. He shot a few rounds in the ceiling, blindly attempting to shoot Arturo. He gasped and sputtered. His eyes then turned white, and his body grew limp. Arturo moved the man off him and opened the classroom door. There, he saw little

Rosie gazing upon him with horrified teary eyes. She ran to Arturo. Her red hair and little arms engulfed Arturo as she sobbed violently into his shoulder. He caressed her hair and shushed her.

"There, there, my little flower," softly cooed Arturo. "I am here."

Quickly, Arturo carried Rosie and led all the little witches out of the classroom and out of the building. Arturo ushered all the other students out of the building as well. The children ran out of the school as quickly as they could and returned home. Gunshots were still heard in the air. Shouting and screaming continued. Arturo then smelled something. It smelled foul and bitter. Arturo's eyes widened. He grabbed onto little Rosie tightly and began to run.

BOOOOOOOOOOOOM!!!!!!!!!

A wind of hellish fire burst from inside the school. Arturo and Rosie flew out of the building like ragdolls from the blast. Flames roared and hissed as they ate the historic building. Fire waved in the windows. Smoke rose to the sky. Arturo held onto little Rosie. She coughed as she continued sobbing into his chest. Arturo checked her face and her limbs and body for any injuries. She was untouched.

"HARK, PEOPLE OF SALEM!" shouted a loud voice from the top of the burning school. It was one of the armed men. He stood alongside three others with cruel smiles on their faces. The crowd gasped in horror at the men. Soon, a squadron of Salemite police rode through the crowd on their horses. Their horses whinnied in fright as the intense flames consumed the school building.

"HARK, PEOPLE OF SALEM," continued the armed man as he and his friends raised their hands in unison. "MAY GOD SMITE SATAN AND ALL OF THOSE WHO DWELL UPON THIS GODFORSAKEN LAND! MAY GOD WIELD THE MAN OF THE FIELDS! DEUS VULT!"

The men reached into their pockets and pulled out a long rope. They tied it around their necks and to the school's flagpole that waved their flag proudly in the wind. The men then took a step on the edge. The crowd gasped. The men ceremoniously raised their hands to the sky and jumped off the building's ledge.

The crowd screamed in horror. Arturo shielded Rosie from the horrific scene. She continued sobbing into his chest, as he caressed her soft, red hair. He kissed her head, as tears rolled down his cheeks. He looked in horror as the devilish flames engulfed the school. He looked in horror as the flames engulfed the hanging corpses of the armed men. Arturo heard the screams of children inside the building.

Arturo felt numb once again. He turned away from the building and carried little Rosie home. They had an important evening to attend to.

17

The day fell into night. The full moon rose high. The shadows danced their mischievous dances. Arturo stood in front of his mirror, wearing his best pants, loosely fitted shirt, and sandals, as Goody Adamson and Lady Cathleen requested. He fidgeted with his shirt, trying his best to make it straight. He missed his overalls and button-down shirts. But tonight, was a special night that he had to take part in. He had to do it. Screams from the burning building still rang in his ears.

He climbed down the stairs and noticed how the house was completely empty and quiet. In the darkness, the furniture looked sinister, and the walls looked small and tight. Anxiety consumed Arturo as he nervously searched for his hosts and their guests. From the kitchen window, he saw a light–a firelight. He opened the backdoor and saw a group of people around a blazing bonfire. They were all completely naked. The fire possibly reached ten feet tall and provided extra warmth for those standing near it. However, the air was bitter and cold this evening.

The individuals looked familiar. Arturo squinted and noticed that they were all the guests from the Summer Solstice he met on the balcony. The noble politicians danced and waved their arms and heads around. They were all covered in blood. They all sang strange words. In the darkness of the forest behind them, he stood in awe with such a ritual. They soon began chanting louder and louder. They cackled and laughed. A sharpened stick and a chalice appeared at his feet. He took the stick and the chalice. He held it and admired it. The chalice was beautiful and ornate. It tingled his fingers when he had the chalice. Something compelled Arturo to drink from it. He desired its sweetness. His mouth began to water with desire. Without hesitating, Arturo drank from it.

Immediately, Arturo felt light-headed, as if he had lost control. He heard the sound of a drum. He felt the rhythm in his feet. He couldn't help but move around. He felt so free and liberated. Soon his clothes were removed, and he danced freely into the night. He felt a rush of sweet, pure ecstasy surge through him. He felt the sweet embrace of the shadow. He felt its warmness on his naked body. Arturo danced around the mighty flames with the witches. He cocked his head, waved his arms, and screamed at the top of his lungs their chants.

With blurred vision, Arturo saw a man strapped in chains against a stone altar. Arturo and the other witches danced around the altar in celebration, continuing their screams and cackles of the night. Goody Adamson put out her arms and shouted in a crazed cackle, *"Tonight, we celebrate not only the Devil's Sabbath but also the beginning of a new era for our nation! We have found the one prophesied to destroy us once and for all! We have finally found him, and he is here with us tonight!"*

Still, in a fit of ecstasy, Arturo tried to wake himself from this trance. His vision blurred. He tried pinching himself, but he couldn't move his arms. He told himself that he had to run away before they killed him. Arturo thought of every possible way to escape them, but all resulted in him being killed immediately. His feet and body cemented themselves to the grass. His body did not feel like his. He felt as if he had been possessed by the Horned Father himself.

"*I present to you the prophesied one!*" announced Goody Adamson, with wild eyes. "*He was a Catholic Traveler and was just imported and captured a few months ago! He has proven to be the one who will destroy us! He has admitted that he is the chosen one sent by the enemy to put our great nation into flames! I give to you, brothers and sisters of the night, the man of prophecy himself: Giuseppe Alessandro!*"

Arturo's vision soon cleared, and there was an obviously drugged Pino, his body laying loosely, chained to the altar. Arturo began to scream in his head, but he could not open his lips and allow the pitiful sounds of sadness and anger to escape. He had to save Pino.

"*I must ask Salem's greatest crusader to draw the first blood,*" announced Goody Adamson, noticing the strange object in Arturo's hand. "*It appears that the Horned Father has given you the weapon of his choice. If you will, Doctor. Please do us the greatest honor of sacrificing the Man of the Fields."*

Arturo's body then lunged forward. He felt his body was a marionette again. Streams of tears trickled his face. He looked to the sky and saw that his hands were raised, holding the pointed stick that the shadow had given him. He looked at Pino. Pino then turned his head loosely towards Arturo.

"Arturo, please," Pino said hoarsely, tears streaming down his face. "You can't do this, old boy. You can't do this. You are my friend. You are my brother. I beg you. Please. Remember who you are! You are not like them! You are not a man of the Devil nor the Inquisition. You are a man that will save us. A man of goodness. Remember, old boy: *Benedictus pacis.*"

Arturo's arms lunged downwards. Blood erupted from Pino's heart. Pino gasped for a few moments. His eyes widened in shock and despair. A single tear fell as he gazed into Pino's eyes. He gave one last final breath and collapsed. Arturo then collapsed onto the grass.

Arturo felt a collection of bodies on top of him, caressing, kissing, and feeling. His eyes were still wide. He felt the witches' breath and hands all over him. Goody Adamson went on top of him and looked at him with eyes of desire. She then leaned over and kissed him on the lips softly. Arturo screamed, but no sound could escape his lips. His body had gone completely limp. Moans of desire filled the evening. The fire roared with fury and anger. Blood soaked the ground beneath the orgy of witches. Arturo felt a surge of anger, sadness, and shame throughout his body as if struck by lightning. His body remained unmoved as he was molested by his witch captors. He looked to the empty sky. With a single tear falling to his cheek, he asked the sky,

"Why me, Father? Why me?"

Arturo's vision then turned to black.

18

Arturo stood on top of a pile of rubble, what was once St. Peter's Basilica. A sour breeze of sulfur reached Arturo's nose. The holy house had completely fallen. The city was completely silent. Silence hung in the air, as did the rebels in their nooses. Corpses decorated the streets and the blood painted them. Fire blazed as Arturo carefully observed his surroundings in case any potential rebels had survived and were combing off any remaining Samuelites. Silence still remained. He was alone.

Arturo climbed the steps of the former basilica. The building was destroyed. Pews were burned to charcoal. Murals and pictures were completely torn. Bullet holes scattered the walls. Statues were graffitied grotesquely with crude colors. Bodies of Samuelites and rebels carpeted the basilica floors. The beauty of the church had been completely erased. All except the altar itself. The crucifix of Christ hung loosely under a single

216

wire. Christ looked upon His house and Arturo with pity. His

children had completely destroyed His home.

Arturo knelt in respect when approaching the holy

ground. He gave the sign of the cross and removed his Samuelite

helmet. He dropped it on the floor with a hard thud. The thud

echoed throughout the basilica. He turned towards the direction

of the echoes for a slight moment. When he averted his eyes

towards the altar, a single door appeared. It was a simple door

made of acacia, the trees that stood outside of Johannesburg. It

had a golden doorknob with the image of a sunflower on it.

Arturo approached the door and opened it.

Outside of the door, he stood in a field that he had never

seen before. The grass was tall and beautiful. A group of poppies

sprouted as he walked. The cool breeze kissed his bloodied

cheeks softly. He gazed upon the wildlife. The smell of earth

came to Arturo. He heard the songbirds singing their mating

calls. He then saw a large stone that stood next to the tree. The

rock trickled with blood. On top of the rock was the head of a bloodied black goat. Flies buzzed and ate its eyes as its tongue

fell loosely over its lips. Arturo gasped in horror.

***

Arturo opened his eyes. He stared at a brown wooden

ceiling. Arturo was lying in a warm bed of hay. He itched and

scratched. He then got up and rubbed his eyes in exhaustion.

When he rose, a surge of pain shot through his temples. He

groaned. He rubbed his temple to alleviate his pain. His hands

felt wet and warm. Arturo then looked at his hands and saw that

he was completely covered in blood. Next to him was a black

mass of fur. Arturo screamed. He saw it was the body of the

black goat. The black goat's head was driven through a wooden

stake. Flies swarmed around his eyes and began eating the flesh

of the sacred creature. Arturo felt a sharp object poking at his

side. He picked it up and observed it. It was a bloodied dagger.

The barn door swung open. A young boy wearing a red

cap, white shirt, and brown shorts with no shoes entered the

barn. In his hand, he held a bucket of feed. The boy's eyes

widened, and he dropped the bucket. He froze like a deer trying to paralyze itself from its hunter. The boy then ran out the barn door quickly with a flash.

"*THE HORNED FATHER IS DEAD!*" he shouted. "*THE HORNED FATHER IS DEAD! THE HORNED FATHER IS DEAD!*"

Arturo chased the boy out of the barn, still holding the knife in hand. The boy ran towards the marketplace. Crowds of people bartered and sold their goods early in the morning. Arturo ran towards the boy, but he was swift. Arturo couldn't keep up. The boy kept screaming, his cap falling off his head, his eyes stunned with fright as the naked, crazed, bloody, mustached man chased him. The boy then climbed on top of the roof of a stand. He shouted at the top of his lungs and pointed at Arturo:

"*THE HORNED FATHER IS DEAD! THE HORNED FATHER IS DEAD! HELP! HE KILLED THE HORNED FATHER.*"

All the Salemites in the marketplace then grew incredibly silent. They all turned and glared at Arturo. Within seconds, hundreds of hands, big and small, smooth and rough, clawed and dangerous, grabbed at Arturo. He punched and kicked him and grabbed him by the hair. One woman tried to pull his mustache, but she was thankfully out of arm's reach. They shouted and cursed at him. They all then carried Arturo up the steps of the temple. They burst through the temple doors and knelt Arturo before the council. The mob shouted in great fury.

"What is the meaning of all this?!" shouted a bewildered Goody Adamson.

"This man killed the Horned Father, high priestess! He killed our Lord!" shouted a man from the crowd.

"Let's kill him! He must pay!" shouted a young woman. The mob shouted and cheered in agreement.

"SILENCE!!!" shouted Goody Adamson standing from her elevated seat. *"I will not tolerate such insolence in this room. Given our history of wrongful accusations from our forefather's enemies, we do have laws of proper judge and jury. We must assess this man the proper way. The council must assess what exactly happened. Where is the witness?"* Goody Adamson gave

Arturo a look of absolute hate and betrayal. Next to her, little Rosie sat in horror.

"*I am the witness, m'lady!*" shouted a small voice. The boy in the red cap went through the mob with his hand raised high above his little head.

"*Do you swear under the name of the Horned Father, the Council before you, and to the good people of Salem and this land, that you are telling the whole truth?*" asked Goody Adamson.

"*I swear it.*"

"*Then proceed, young man.*"

"*Well, my family and I have been assigned since our landing here in Salem to take care of the Horned Father's physical form. My father has done it and his father before him. I take care of the Horned Father. I tend to his hay, clean his waste, and make sure he is well-fed with the finest mead and vegetables.*"

"*Do go on,*" urged Goody Adamson.

"This morning, I came to the Horned Father's sacred home, just as I have always done. I opened the door, and I saw this man lying next to the dead body of the Horned Father."

"I have housed this man for months, boy," said Goody Adamson. *"He is completely harmless. He wouldn't even hurt the hair of my familiar, let alone our Lord's physical body. He saved my daughter and her classmates from the terrorist attack at the city's school. How do we know it was this man and this man alone?"*

"Because he carried this dagger with him," the boy said as he unsheathed the bloodied dagger. The dagger shined and glittered with red, as did Arturo. The mob gasped in horror.

"This is an absolute lie, Goody Adamson!" shouted Arturo with outrage. "I am completely innocent! I would never do such a thing to harm your sacred animal!"

"That is High Priestess Adamson, to you, Dr. Butera," growled Adamson. *"You are covered in the Horned Father's blood, Doctor. The evidence speaks for itself. You have killed the Horned Father. It shames me that you were openly welcomed*

with open arms by not only my family but the people of Salem.

Because the crime is beyond even this council's control, Dr.

Arturo Butera, under the name of this council, you will be sent to

the Sisters of Old themselves to determine your fate. May they

have mercy on your soul."

"No," begged Arturo. "You don't understand! I am

innocent! I am–" Rosie's face turned bright red as she held her

mother, sobbing. She took one last look at Arturo and was utterly

mortified by the scene. A sack went over Arturo's head, and all

he saw was the black unknown.

19

A cool gust of wind entered the dark, cobble-stoned room. The room was completely empty. Arturo dangled upside down from the ceiling from a chain around his heels. The room was completely dark, with no candlelight in sight. A bag still covered his head. The hot air inside the bag made him dizzy and nauseous. His voice was hoarse after hours of screaming for help, trying to declare his innocence. His body shivered as he hung upside down entirely naked. He felt exposed. He prayed for security. He prayed that Pino would come to save him from this mess. He wished that his brave brother would come back and save him from the clutches of his devil-worshiping captors. But now Pino was dead. He kicked and twisted his legs.

"Be still, my young prince," said a strange yet ancient voice.

"You will only make those shackles tighter," said another strange voice.

"There is no way for you to escape," said a third voice.

"Who are you?" asked Arturo angrily. "Reveal yourself to me! I demand to know my enemies' faces!"

The three voices cackled in unison.

"Such a brave and foolish boy..." said the first voice.

"...you will not die quickly..." said the second voice.

"...unless you submit to us," said the third voice.

"Submit to you?" angrily spat Arturo under his hood. "I have already submitted to you, Adamson, and the city of Salem! What more do you want from me? I didn't kill that stupid goat!"

The voices cackled again.

"We do not care for the false prophet..." said the first voice.

"...we only care for you..." said the second voice.

"...the Man of the Fields..." said the third voice.

"Who in the hell are you?!" shouted Arturo, losing his patience. "I demand to know who you are! Remove my hood at once!"

Arturo then felt a pair of long nails trail from his stomach, chest, and neck. Arturo shivered. The nails felt like rusted nails. The sack then flew off his head. Arturo's vision was disoriented, but he adjusted. He looked around and wiggled his body. He winced as the shackles tightened even more. He looked around the room and saw three pairs of glowing eyes staring at him. Torches around the room ignited at once, revealing three ugly hags standing before Arturo.

"I am Gala the Elder," said the first hag.

"I am Aoife the Wise," said the second hag.

"And I am Liadain the Gifted. We are the Sisters of Old. Keepers of the Satanic Law and the Commonwealth of the Horned Father. We are the rulers of America."

"I don't believe this. I was brought here for you to judge my fate over a crime I did not commit! I am innocent, I tell you!" declared Arturo.

"Oh, you silly stupid boy! You cry like a babe!" said Gala, annoyed.

"We do not care for the stupid goat!" said Aoife.

"It was only a weapon for us to yield to our benefit!" shouted Liadain.

"It was for power, wasn't it?" questioned Arturo. "You had the 'physical embodiment of the Horned Father' as a ploy to control the people of Salem and the rest of this Godforsaken nation? It was all a lie!"

"Such tools are necessary when time continues," angrily spat Gala. "Iron and machines have replaced faith. It was only necessary that we had to cement the power of the Horned Father through physical belief. Salem has lost its old ways! The Horned Father is angry at us and punishes us! We must battle the

Catholics and their kin. He will abandon us unless we restore order! The prophecy will become true unless we act now!"

"The prophecy of the Man of the Fields," answered Arturo.

"Yes. The Man of the Fields will destroy not just our nation but all nations as far as the farthest reaches of the world, with fire far greater than the lowest depths of Hell. You, my little prince, are the Man of the Fields. You wield a weapon far greater than divine comprehension. You must tell us your secret."

"I don't know what you are talking about," lied Arturo. "I am not the man that you are speaking of."

Gala then grabbed a chunk of his long, dark hair and yanked it downwards. Arturo winced with pain. The witch shook his head roughly to be still. With her long, rusted nails, Gala poked at the back of Arturo's ear.

"You bear the mark of the prophecy," said Gala. "Your little friend has told you: 'Birthmarks mean important things.' Birthmarks can determine your faith, boy. They determine what will happen to you and who you will become. You, my boy, are a man of a prophecy. You are the end of the world unless you help us. We know you wield the weapon: the Hammer of God."

"We are interested in your technology, Doctor," said Liadain. "We know who you are, Arturo Mattei. We have heard stories of your family. Your family is legendary! Your family has brought fear to the hearts of this nation for centuries. We know of your legacy as the world's greatest mind and inventor. We know what the weapon you hold is capable of. Our alchemists from our nation and Indigenous allies are incredibly interested in your device."

"You can help us dominate the world against the Inquisition!" said Aoife. "Think of all the lands we can conquer! The people we will save! We will liberate them!"

"Yes, liberate them. That way, you can force them to be subjected to your Satanic doctrine!" shouted Arturo, his face turning red. "You are no better than the Inquisition itself! You silence those who present the truth. They want the same power you hold! They hold the same beliefs you hold. They, too, will

229

blindly kill anyone for their God and maintain their power. You hold nothing but petty grudges and wish to conquer lands in the name of power, freedom, and religion. My device is a weapon of madness and destruction. Life is meant to be saved and protected, not destroyed. You and the Inquisition will continue to send innocent lives to fight your wars without consequence. Every life is precious. I made a vow to save lives, not conquer them. With that, I refuse to help you."

The witches cackled and squealed.

"Such a brave, brave soldier," said Gala. "Life is not as precious as you may think! People are born, used, and die. Your logic is flawed, Doctor. Think of it like this: a colony of ants wants to swim across a perilous stream. They create a boat shape using the bodies of other living ants within their colony. The ants on top are safe and secure. Yet the ones being the base of the vessel ultimately drown. They sacrifice their lives for the sake of their colony. That way, the queen and the rest of the colony could survive.

There is no ultimate point in saving people, Doctor. There will always be ant queens that will use their subjects to sail across the perilous journey of war and death. You can't save everyone, little prince. People are meant to be ruled and die for their nations. We are bred that way. Being good is ultimately pointless if you risk your life to save everyone, especially people who will not think of protecting you. People are selfish and only fight for their own beliefs and survival. They are savages. Without power and control, there will be chaos. That is why we must rule and control who lives and who dies. Your beliefs are flawed, Doctor."

Arturo thought long and hard. Silence hung in the air as he did.

"You are wrong, m'lady," he countered confidently. "You are completely wrong. Are you aware of the story of Samson? In my faith, Samson was a flawed individual who boasted about the superhuman strength that God gave him. He was fooled by his hubris and the affections of a woman that came from the same group of his enemies. He learns his lesson

231

but ultimately dies by crumbling the palace, crushing himself and his enemies. He sacrificed himself, m'lady. His own people and his enemies were flawed people, yet Samson still sacrificed himself to save his people."

"You cannot save everyone, Doctor," said Gala, her green eyes flashing.

"By God, I will," said Arturo sharply.

"Interesting words coming from a citizen of the Inquisition," said Liadain.

"I am no longer Inquisition nor Salemite. I belong to no one. I am a man of life. I am a man that wants to fight for life and preserve it. We use divinity to define our humanity. We spit on the faces of our gods and use war and violence in their name. We have made faith and life meaningless. I vowed to bring peace to this earth. And by God, I will keep it. To hell with your prophecy."

The witches growled and circled Arturo.

"Choose your words wisely, Doctor," grinned Aoife. "We don't want your family to pay the price for your insolence."

Arturo's face turned from bright red to stark white. "What do you mean?" he said nervously. Suddenly the screams of a familiar voice echoed throughout the room.

"ARTURO! HELP ME!" shouted a familiar female voice.

"PAPA, HELP ME! PLEASE SAVE ME! PAPA!" shouted four small voices.

Arturo shook and stirred from his chains. They were the voices of his wife and children! His family!

"Leave my family out of this, you filthy hags!" Arturo said as his shackles rattled viciously. "You let my wife and children go! Take me instead! I beg you!"

The witches continued circling around him like a pack of wolves cornering their injured prey. They cackled and motioned around him. They pushed Arturo's hanging body like a swing.

He spun and swung loosely. He swore and cursed the three sisters.

"My dear boy, you said you are a man of life!" cackled Gala maniacally. "With life comes blood, and with blood comes a price!"

"You must pay for the lives of your family!" hissed Aoife.

"Or they will die the most gruesome death!" sneered Liadain. "They will beg for us to end their lives quickly!"

"However, you can have your family under one condition, Doctor," said Gala mysteriously.

"What else do you want from me?" spat Arturo angrily.

"You can always...sign his book," grinned Gala.

"You could never get me to sign that book!" Arturo roared. "You will have to sign my name with my cold dead hands to get a signature out of me!"

"Think of it, Doctor. You can help our nation and answer to our demands, and you can have your family, and we can release you," said Aoife. "Or you can refuse our proposal and we will kill your family."

"My answer is still no, hag," said Arturo defiantly.

"Very well," said Gala, shrugging. The chain then dropped, and Arturo fell roughly to the ground. He moaned in pain. His vision was blurred, and he saw the witches' shapes dance before his eyes within the dim firelight. Arturo then saw a shiny gold object clunk onto the cobblestone pavement. He felt it reach his feet. He picked it up and squinted to observe the strange object. He blinked until his vision cleared. It was a gold box. Within the box were strange objects. He picked up a bloody ring. He looked closer. It was Antoinetta's wedding ring. He then picked up a metal wind-up bird and horse all covered in blood. He gasped in horror and began to weep softly.

"You now have nothing to live for, Doctor," cooed Aoife. "You are the only one who can escape their fate. Will you sign the book?"

Arturo wiped his tears and nodded. A pen and an archaic leather-bound book appeared before him out of thin air. Arturo's tears landed on the papyrus sheets of paper. He dried his tears. Arturo signed the Devil's book.

"Congratulations, Doctor! Welcome to the beginning of victory for Salem! For America! We will smite the enemy, dear doctor. We will smite them all starting with this."

Gala then placed a small trinket into Arturo's open hands and closed them. Arturo opened his hands. It was the pocket watch.

"The authorities found that under your floorboards, Dr. Mattei. We wouldn't want a dangerous device in a house where a family lives. You will help us, Doctor. You will make hundreds of these weapons as mighty as the Lady of the Lake! Lead us to victory, Doctor. Lead us to victory."

20

The sun glistened brightly, gently reflecting off the beautiful waters of the Mediterranean. The waves gently crashed to and fro on the soft, sugar-white sandy beaches. The gulls called in the sky. The laughter of children filled the blue, cloudless sky. On top of a small hill by the shores of the sea, stood a modest, yet beautiful cottage. There, Arturo Mattei and his beloved wife, Antoinetta, sat on a blanket as they watched their children play in the crystal blue water. Arturo and Antoinetta giggled to each other, enjoying their children's innocence and fun.

Arturo laid his head on Antoinetta's lap. She played with his hair as she gave him sweet little kisses on his lips. He playfully roared and grabbed her angelic small face and playfully pretended to eat her cheeks, giving her a million kisses. Antoinetta laughed and screamed with glee. They wrestled each other and laughed with pure joy.

"Unhand me, you strange man!" said Antoinetta
playfully.

"Never, until my gorgeous wife lets me...eat her!" said
Arturo as he began pretending to nibble on Antoinetta, tickling
her with his mustache.

"Stop! Stop! I have so much to live for!"

"Oh I know but I can't help it! I am so, so hungry!"

Antoinetta playfully smacked and punched her husband.
"Oh stop! Not in front of the children!"

"They are by the shore," said Arturo, brushing
Antoinetta's hair out of her eyes. "They are completely fine!
Look how much fun they are having!"

"Yes, they are. You made the right decision moving back
home, darling. The children absolutely love it here."

"Thank you, my love. I just couldn't stand being in
Rome. With the Inquisition breathing down my neck, I just
needed some time away. Coming back home to Cassino felt like
the right thing to do."

Arturo got up and stared into the ocean. He saw a group

of gulls wading in the water as the gentle waves waded towards

the shore. Arturo smelled the salty air and sighed.

"Annie, I still don't feel well. I am still not happy here. I

just feel like I am needed elsewhere."

"Where else would we go, darling? Where would you

like to go? England, Japan, Egypt, Switzerland? We can go

anywhere, my love. I just want you to be happy for us. I see it.

The children see it. Three days ago, Anita said that she saw you

staring at a photo of Roberto for hours in the workshop. She said

you didn't tinker or do any of your usual work. I understand you

need help but let me help you. I know there are doctors that can

help you with this sort of thing. A procedure given to soldiers

who come back home!"

"No, Annie. There's nothing you can really do. The

dreams are getting worse as time goes on. The last thing I need

is to be some cheery vegetable. I don't want to lose myself even

more, my love. I just need to find something that will help me,

that way everything will be normal in my life. I am just lacking

purpose. I found a purpose when I was with Roberto. I wanted to

239

be a knight like him when I worked for the force in Rome, but
that still led me to nothing. I think God is just laughing at me at
this point."

"That is not true! And I know, my love, but I will be here
for you! I love you, Arturo. You are mine always."

"And you are mine, Annie. But I think I found the
answer to my problems. But I am not sure if you are going to like
it."

Antoinetta gave an expression of concern. Her long,
dark hair blew in the salty wind, as she looked at Arturo with her
big, beautiful eyes. Her cheeks were rosy and sweet, but her lips
gave a whimper of sadness for her husband. "What is it,
Arturo?" she said inquisitively, as the waves crashed in the
distance.

"I was in town the other day and I wanted to go to the
pub and have some time for myself. I was having an absolutely
awful day. I had a dream about Roberto and what happened at
the Chesapeake. I went to have a drink and you know how much
I loathe drinking. I don't know what came over me, but I just felt
the need to have a drink. Anyways, I go to the bartender and I

ask him for a beer. I finish it and then I ask for another. Soon, I
had at least six drinks at this point. I was a complete mess,
yelling and hollering how I am a complete monster and failure to
not only the Inquisition, but my family. I was a sad excuse for a
father and a husband. I couldn't look at myself in the mirror
because I was responsible for Roberto's death. If I wasn't
distracted in the field, he would still be here today.

I drank my cares away and I am standing on the table,
hollering and yelling. No one is able to kick me out because
everyone knows who I am. They know who my family is. If they
so much as speak ill to my face, they fear that the Inquisition will
take them right then and there. They fear me. Everyone does. My
blood is complete filth. It is nothing but fuel for the evil of this
empire that we stand on. My family is the reason why it rains
blood every day. God was gone. He had abandoned me. I felt
hopeless, Annie. I felt hopeless, until I met him.

I was then escorted by this strange man. He had long,
white robes, a turban, and a long gray scarf that covered his
face. The man carried me to the piazza and sat me down at its
center. I acted like a complete fool. I began singing complete

nonsense and then cried like a child. I felt so alone. I collapsed

and promptly vomited. Soon I felt the taste of water enter my

lips. Like an infant, the stranger held me in his arms as he

nursed me with his water. I soon regained consciousness and I

looked at my guardian angel.

He was incredibly tall, had dark eyes, and a great smile.

But the most peculiar feature of my hero was his face. His face

was completely tattooed with fascinating lines that seemed to

have some important meaning. They were so unique yet, he wore

them proudly. He looked fearsome, yet his eyes were warm and

kind. He chuckled to himself as he caressed my head, assuring

me that I will be well-taken care of. I closed my eyes for a

moment and slept for an hour. He held me throughout that hour.

After I awoke, I finally came to my senses and saw that

the strange man was still holding me, watching over me.

Awkwardly, I stood up and thanked the man for his troubles. I

reached over and tried to pay him for his troubles, but he

refused. I asked him if he was a stranger in Cassino. He simply

nodded. I asked him why he was there. He then pulled out from

around his neck a necklace that bore a strange symbol that looked similar to a cross but wasn't. Somehow the cross was

comforting to look at and felt a tingling feeling as I held it in my

hand. I felt a wave of peace wash over me. I asked him who he

was, and he said that he was part of a missionary group called

the Travelers. They are these incredible people that work outside

of the Inquisition that travel to places where people truly need

them. They give an oath of pacifism and go on a two-year

mission anywhere around the world! Immediately, I felt light on

my feet. I begged him to tell me more. He then proceeded to tell

me all about his missions and that he even went beyond his two-

year mission and was a Traveler for 15 years! With all these

stories that he told, stories of enlightenment and joy, I felt whole

again. Darling, I want to be a Traveler."

Tears streamed down Antoinetta's beautiful face and her

lips quivered. She covered her face and began to cry. Arturo

then brought her to his chest and caressed her hair. He hushed

and consoled her. Tears began to stream down his face as well.

They both began to cry.

"Arturo, I don't know if I can handle this. I love you so much. But, darling, we have four children! I can't raise them by myself. I don't know what to do! I am so scared."

"Annie, I know but I am barely a father to my children, let alone a husband. You have been suffering for years! I have been suffering for years, my love. I want to be whole for you! This is my calling by God! Ever since I first laid eyes on you, I promised God that I would be the best husband for you. I would take care of you and my children with my heart and soul. But, darling, I think this will help us so much. I want to be whole again."

Antoinetta sniffled for a few moments. Arturo brought out a handkerchief from his breast pocket and wiped his wife's tears. She giggled through her tears and kissed him. Passion and love filled both their hearts.

"Ok, Arturo. You can go on this mission trip, but you need to promise me two things: first, you can only do two years and two years only, and second, you must come home as soon as possible."

"For you, my love, the whole world! Whatever you say I'll do it! I have enough money saved for us that will last us years while I am gone. I don't even know how to thank you."

"You can thank me by writing to me and the children."

"Yes! I will write to you and the kids every day! I'll even send them little wind ups that way they always know I am thinking of them! I swear, my love, I will return a new man! God will bless us and this family forever! I love you, Annie."

"And I love you more, Arturo."

She then kissed her husband and smiled. Arturo was excited for the new journey that was coming for him. He felt new and whole. He was ready to find himself and fulfill his destiny. He was ready to be the hero his brother always wanted to be. He would do it for his family! For Roberto! For God! He was ready for his adventure. The sun began to set as the darkness consumed the ocean. A storm began to roll from the distance. The beauty had disappeared. Arturo was uncertain what the future would hold.

***

Arturo awoke from his dream. He was in a simple room. It possessed a simple cot, a desk, worktable, and dining table. A bundle of clothes sat on a stool. He dressed. The walls were decorated with stone and curtains. Arturo marveled at the very structure of the castle. Above him was a small window that he had to tiptoe to reach. One would not necessarily say it was a room with a view. Arturo looked out the window and saw the Atlantic Ocean meeting the buzzing metropolis of Salem.

Arturo sat in his cot in absolute shame. He had sold his soul to the Devil. He had lost not only his soul but everything. He had lost his best friend, comrades, children, and beautiful wife. Arturo put his hands in his face and cried softly. He felt lost. He felt alone. No one was with him. No one was watching over him nor holding him or comforting him. He was utterly alone. Arturo then looked up, got on his knees, and folded them in prayer.

"Lord, why have you forsaken me?" pleaded Arturo. "Why do you watch me suffer? What more can you take away from me? You have taken away my home, my friends, my family! You have taken away my life! I am nothing but a puppet for politicians, yet you do nothing. I try to do your work. I saved the people of Johannesburg. I saved my countrymen. I betrayed them and saved other nations. Yet, I am in prison working for your enemy because you have not saved me."

Tears streamed down Arturo's face. His face felt hot, and he clenched his hands until he made indentations on his knuckles with his fingernails.

"Forgive me, Lord. I am yours and yours only. I do not walk among any kingdom besides your kingdom. I do not serve any king besides you. I am your servant. Let me be a beacon of hope. I am the Man of the Fields. Guide me to do what is right. Guide me to—"

BOOOOOOOOOOOOM!!!!!!!!!

Arturo flew across the room. He pulled over his desk and used it as a shield. Dust and rubble filled the air. Rocks and pebbles were scattered around the room. He dusted himself and rubbed his eyes. It was a cannonball. Arturo's eyes widened, and his mouth gaped in absolute horror.

A fleet of one hundred metal ships sailed across the Atlantic as the castle overlooked their visitors. The ships waved a familiar flag. It was the flag of the Inquisition. The war had begun.

21

Hope blasted through Arturo's window. Hundreds of ships fired at the shore as American ships sailed to rally the Inquisitional warships. The metal warships fired at will and decimated the American forces with incredible ease. Arturo could hear the screams of fear and panic within Salem. Cries of women and children hung in the air. Thousands of witches flew west away from the war-torn metropolis. Smoke rose to the dark sky, and flames of hell illuminated the roofs of the skyscrapers.

Arturo's mind began to flow with ideas of how to safely escape this wretched castle. He looked down the window to scale the height of the castle. It was approximately fifty feet above the ground. He looked around the room for possible items to makeshift as a sort of device that could help him climb safely down. He then noticed a pair of coat hooks. An idea surged through him like lightning. The feeling of lightness reached his toes. His mustache twitched with cleverness and delight. Arturo then wrapped a pair of his bedsheets and the wall curtains into a rope. Thankfully, his room hung a dozen long curtains. He wrapped the end of his makeshift to his chest and grappled the coat hook to the most secure edge of the blown window. Arturo then put his pocket watch around his neck. He tapped it to ensure it was in place. It was secure. He then began to climb down.

Arturo ran through the thick forest. Shots of cannons and gunfire were heard in the distance. The sounds of birds and other animals filled the arboreal atmosphere. He noticed how flocks of birds flew to the ocean, fleeing the land across the sea. He saw a herd of deer run gracefully through the thick brush, passing Arturo with urgency. Arturo knew he was on a mission. He clutched the device tightly. He had to journey on.

Arturo ran until he saw a bright light through the dark force. He saw a clearing where he could finally escape the clutches of both the Inquisition and Salem. He can live away in secret and remain a hermit within the American forest for the rest of his days. He could hide away in the sacred Rocky Mountains that Arturo saw in the Salemite temple mural on his first day. He began daydreaming of absolute peace and quiet. He would live as a guardian for the rest of his days protecting the world from the wretched device. Peace would remain while nations aimlessly try to defend themselves. Hope was certain!

A sudden crashing of trees and bushes erupted behind him. The roar of an engine was close. Arturo ducked for cover. A gigantic blur of white and black emerged from the brush, almost running over Arturo. The mighty vehicle went over him, barely crushing him. Arturo lifted himself from the ground. He noticed a group of armored men exiting the truck. They all wore white armored uniforms. They all had a strange cross symbol inside a circle branded onto their foreheads. They each pulled a lever, and the trucks began to transform. The cargo shell began to open, slowly revealing a pointed structure. The men then set up what appeared to be a control station and began their work. In the distance, Arturo saw a very familiar figure commanding these strange men. The familiar soldier turned and glared at Arturo with familiar hawk-like eyes that could pierce the hearts of its victims. It was Commander Octavian.

"Dr. Mattei!" shouted Commander Octavian. "I never thought I would see you again! I thought you were surely killed by the Weird Sisters! Pleasure for you to join the show!"

"What on earth are you doing, Octavian," growled Arturo. "What is the meaning of all this?"

"Looks like the doctor has grown some balls," laughed Octavian. "Boy, have those fucking witch-breed toughened you up! You were quite the nancy boy when I first met you. Do you know where we are, Dr. Mattei?"

Arturo fumed with anger, but Octavian continued on.

"Well, I'll tell you given how angry you must be. We are at Gallows Hill. Some people don't know what Gallows Hill is. Shit, not even the fucking hags know what this place is! This here, doc, is the exact place where it all started! All those damn Puritans and conquistadors hanging and burning all those witches! It happened right here on this hallowed ground! But today, we are going to put down our silly swords and finally start this war!"

"Enough games! What is the meaning of all this madness? What is this device you are launching?!"

"This here vamp? Why Doctor, it's the future! A future that *you* have started! This beauty is what I call a missile!"

"You're kidding!"

"You got it, doc! Imagine that: a gigantic nuclear bullet that can travel thousands of miles away in minutes! This baby here will be making a one-way trip to Vatican City! The Vatican will then assume that the witches have developed weaponry similar to your device, and they, too, will develop plans for nuclear annihilation. The oceans will finally flow red with the blood of all nations! The world will burn! My brothers and I will finally begin what we have started!"

"You've completely gone mad! You are nothing but a traitor to your own people, Octavian! You're a goddamn witch! You worship the Devil! Pino and I saw you and your little ritual on the *Archangel*! You betray the Inquisition!"

Octavian then removed his mask and threw it to the ground. He then began laughing hysterically. Octavian revealed his face. He looked at Arturo with a menacingly large grin. His teeth were straight and white. He looked incredibly handsome. However, his face looked completely scarred, as if he had bathed in fire. His gray eyes blazed in a fury of madness as he continued laughing.

"You're a goddamn fool, Arturo! I am not a witch! Hell, I do not worship Christ nor the Devil! I simply use the powers of the unknown to help me and my brothers watch the world turn to dust. How do you think I figured out how to build your weapon? Who killed the black goat and left it without a trace? It was all me from the beginning. We were created by dust, and we will turn the world to dust again! My brothers and I have made a pact to destroy nations, ensure war, and spill blood. We hide in the shadows. You are the puppets, and we are your masters. We are the Shadowed Hand. Today you will be the last to know about us."

"By God, you won't."

"Sir, we have initiated the countdown!" shouted one of the men. Soon the group of men began kneeling, unsheathed their swords, and opened their arms, muttering strange words.

"My destiny must be fulfilled, Doctor," Commander Octavian said, kneeling, unsheathing his own sword. "Surely, you will understand that. Goodbye, Dr. Mattei. See you in Hell."

Octavian raised his hands and began muttering strange words alongside his comrades. He then closed his eyes and plunged his sword directly into his abdomen. The commander then gave a long groan. His face began to turn red. He then looked up at Arturo and smiled. Octavian collapsed. He was dead.

Arturo ran towards the control stations, pressed as many buttons, and pulled as many switches as he could. He tried to hotwire the controls, but it was completely useless. He then tried typing dozens of different potential combinations for the launch code, but the launch codes were already set. There was no way to cancel the launch. The world was going to end as he knew it.

Arturo felt the tall grass. It tickled his fingertips as they brushed past him. Arturo then knelt and witnessed the beauty of the heavens. Birds chirped sweetly. Then Arturo looked to the ground and saw a single poppy sprouting next to him. He held it close to him and embraced it in his hand. Thoughts of Pino came to mind. His best friend, his ally, his spiritual brother. Pino was always with him until the very end. Even when separated, Pino still prayed for Arturo. He prayed for him because he loved him. He loved him like no person before. They were brothers of God. Arturo looked up. Beauty reigned in the skies.

He saw the sky change from purple to pink and then pink to orange. He pictured his wife and children kneeling next to him. He pictured his beloved Antoinetta at his side and his children at his feet. He imagined seeing his children's shining smiles. He pictured kissing the soft lips of his beloved wife. He held his sweetheart tightly and felt a warmth of love swell over him. He imagined holding them and embracing them as the colors of the sky transformed. Beauty reigned in the skies.

Arturo himself looked at the sunrise. A single tear shed, yet he smiled his mischievous small smile.

He knew what he had to do.

He took out his pocket watch and opened it. He twisted the watch's crown and moved the minute hand to the combination:

12 – 07 – 1909

It was the day his brother died. The day his spirit died. However, Arturo's soul didn't die. Today, his soul blossomed.

Arturo then pressed the center of the pocket watch. The watch began to tick with life. The missiles whirred as they prepared to launch. Arturo patiently waited. He continued looking out at the beautiful sky. It began to turn bright orange.

A different beauty, a brighter light, reigned in the skies....

About the Author

Henry F. Wilde is the author of his debut novel, *Man of the Fields: The Next Crusade for Salem*. Wilde loves to watch science fiction and fantasy films, as well as historical documentaries. He is also an avid collector of vintage science fiction and horror novels. He credits Frank Herbert, Denis Villeneuve, and Francisco Goya for being his visionary inspirations. He lives in Eastern Michigan with his family.

Made in United States
Troutdale, OR
07/26/2024

21540843R00159